I0458212

THE CORPSE FACTORY

WILDSIDE PRESS

WEIRD-MENACE #1

THE CORPSE FACTORY - Weird Menace Classics # 1 -
    $5 per copy.
edited and published by Robert Weinberg, 10606 S. Central
Park, Chicago, Il. 60655

ACKNOWLEDGMENTS

THE CORPSE FACTORY by Arthur Leo Zagat, copyright © 1934
by Popular Publications for Dime Mystery, May 1934.
Copyright renewed 1962. Reprinted by permission of Mrs.
Ruth Zagat

THE CANYON OF MISSING BRIDES by Arthur J. Burks, copyright
© 1937 by Popular Publications for Terror Tales, Nov 1937.
Copyright renewed 1965. Reprinted by permission of Mrs.
Ruth Burks

GODDESS OF EVIL REVELRY by Frederick C. Davis, copyright
© 1936 by Popular Publications for Dime Mystery, Dec. 1936.
Copyright renewed 1964. Reprinted by permission of Frederick C. Davis.

BEAUTY BORN IN HELL by Mindret Lord, copyright © 1939
by Popular Publications for Horror Stories, August 1939.
Copyright renewed 1967. Reprinted by arrangement with
Forrest J. Ackerman, 2495 Glendower Ave., Hollywood,
Calif. 90027, agent for the author's estate.

HOUSE OF HORRIBLE LAUGHTER by Ray Cummings, copyright ©
1937 by Popular Publications for Dime Mystery, May 1937.
Copyright renewed 1965. Reprinted by permission of
Forrest J. Ackerman, 2495 Glendower Ave., Hollywood,
Calif. 90027, agent for the estate of Ray Cummings.

FIRST EDITION

CONTENTS

CHAMBER
OF
HORRORS

Welcome to a world far removed from this mundane sphere
of Watergate, Peanuts, and Angola. Return with us to a
less troubled time - a time when there were still isolated towns and vast uncharted reaches where brooding
horrors could exist - where television was yet to be invented, and ignorant townspeople still believed in age
old superstitions. Enter the world of Weird Menace.
      In their own way, the pulp magazines of the first
half of the twentieth century were a perfect reflection
of their time. While the stories were often outrageous,
the themes were rooted in the troubles of the day. And
the solutions and characters were taken from that same
world. This was not a time of anti-heroes or of instant
analysis. Perhaps people were not simpler then, but we
tended to think that they were. And evil was just that
- a dark and terrible thing, that had to be fought against and destroyed.
      The Weird-Menace Pulps were children of the 1930's.
The first of these magazines was DIME MYSTERY, whose
first Weird Menace issue was published in 1933. Popular
Publications soon followed with two more magazines in
the same vein - HORROR STORIES and TERROR TALES. There
were other imitations as well, some lasting for years,
like THRILLING MYSTERY, others only for a few issues.
All of the magazines, however, died with the birth of
a greater horror - a much more realistic one than the

bizarre horrors in the pulp pages - World War Two.
But for a few years, they flourished and entertained.

The key word is entertainment. These stories are
not intended to be anything more than that. They are
absolutely unbelievable - totally unrealistic - but
they are fun. They require a total suspension of belief. The reader has to let the author take him on a
fantastic trip into a strange world of fast action and
gruesome events. In reprinting these stories, we hope
to capture some of the flavor of the horror pulps, but
not only to give the reader some idea of what these
pulps were like, but also to entertain.

In compiling this and future selections, the
editor contacted as many of the authors who wrote for
these magazines as he could find - along with several
estates for those pulp authors who have passed away
during the intervening years. All stories in this
book, and all future books, are authorized reprints,
and payment is being made to the authors for the
stories used. If any of our readers might know of
a horror pulp author who has not been in contact with
us, we would be happy to learn of them - for their
benefit as well as ours and our readers.

In future books, we will be bringing to you more
of the best stories from the Weird Menace pulps. If
you have some favorite story, we'd be interested in
learning it for possible reprinting. We'd also like
to learn from our readers if they prefer short stories,
novelettes, or complete novels - examples of each are
included in this issue. We want to publish what you
want to read, if you will only let us know what you
want.

Now, turn the page, and return to the days when
Ray Cummings, Arthur Leo Zagat, and their brothers in
fear presented ... the best of the Weird Menaces!

                                    Robert Weinberg
                                    January 1977

BEAUTY BORN IN HELL

Sick with despair since his lovely wife had vanished, young Jeff Ellwood covered a routine assignment at the Royal Palace Theater, uncaring . . . until he realized that he was watching a chorus of beautiful girls who stared like zombies—and who danced the last routine his wife had originated!

CHAPTER ONE

Ballet of Death

IT WAS one of those dull nights when every criminal in New York seemed to be either asleep or dead. I was hanging around the police station hoping for something to break for a story, trying to keep myself awake by thinking about Marjorie. A little, flashily-dressed guy came in and wandered uncertainly over to the lieutenant's desk. I followed him,

by
Mindret
Lord

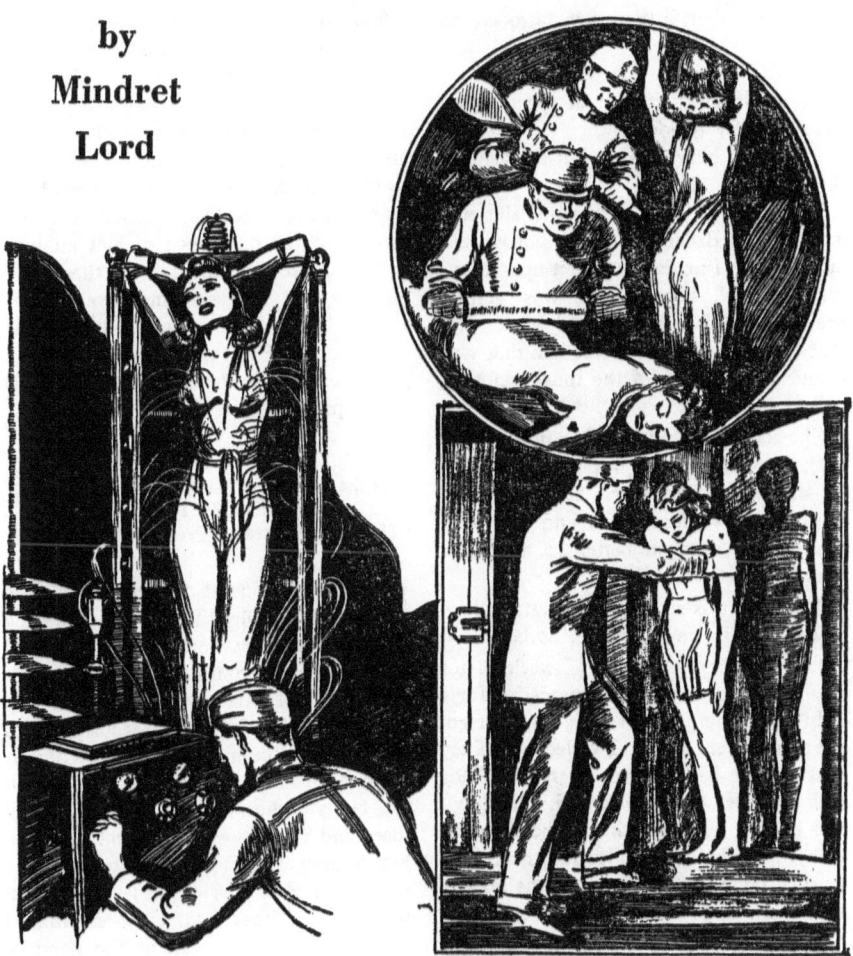

though without feeling much curiosity.

O'Leary looked the little guy over and asked, "Well?"

"Chief, I come to report a missing person." His voice was a tough, Second Avenue whine. "My girl's gone and I want you to find her for me."

"When did you last see her?"

"Tonight—outside the burlesque. She works in the chorus."

O'Leary winked at me. Then he asked, "What makes you think she's disappeared?"

"I know it! I know it because that dame's nuts about me. She wouldn't go nowhere with nobody, unless—" He broke off and dug in his inside coat pocket. "Look. Here's a picture of her."

O'Leary looked at it, then handed it to me. It was a picture of a cheap-looking fat girl in tights; just what you'd expect.

The lieutenant wouldn't take the little guy seriously. He kidded him for awhile and finally told him to go to the Missing Persons Bureau, if she didn't turn up eventually.

When the guy was gone, O'Leary said, "She's given him the air, of course. Did you notice that little heart tattooed on her arm?"

"Yeah," I said.

"Well, if she turns up in the morgue, she'll be easy to identify."

I saw that heart again—but it wasn't in the morgue. . . .

When I first met Marjorie, she was dancing in a Broadway revue, but when I married her, I made her give it up. It was just as well, because she was getting pretty plump for that sort of work. Not that that's a criticsm—I like 'em that way —and she was one of the most beautiful girls I ever saw.

She soon got tired of doing nothing but cook for me and keep our place in order, so she decided to teach stage dancing. Within a few months she had a reputation. She was even better as a teacher than as a dancer.

I tell you this so you'll understand how I was able to find her . . . at last. . . .

One evening, a couple of weeks after that burlesque dame disappeared, Marje didn't come home from her studio. It got later and later; finally I called up. They told me she had started, all right. They had seen her get into a taxi. And that was the last I heard of her. I nearly went crazy, while both the police and the G-men worked on the case. But she was gone— vanished just as completely as if a cyclone had sucked her off the face of the earth.

I'm not going to tell you how I suffered for the next month—you can imagine that. Even the hard-boiled editor of my paper was sorry for me, for he gave me assignments that were calculated to take my mind off the despair, the constant, sick fear that clutched my brain. That's how I happened to be at the Royal Palace for the opening of a new picture and stage show. I was supposed to review it.

I sat there in the dark theatre, not looking at the screen and not caring whether it was a comedy or a tragedy, a wow or a flop. After what seemed like hours, the picture dragged to its mushy close, the orchestra played an overture and the stage show began. It was just like every other stage show that you've ever seen, until the precision dancers came out! There were twenty-four of them as perfectly matched as pearls in a necklace. There couldn't have been the difference of half an inch in height between any two of them, and their figures, besides being lovely, were absolutely similar in size, shape and dimensions. They might all have been plaster casts from the same mold. I looked at my program and read:

NEW! THRILLING!
For the First Time We Are Proud to Present
THE DEVIL'S DARLINGS
The World's Greatest Precision Dance Group

I HAD never heard of them before and I wondered why. When I looked back at the stage, they were in the middle of an intricate tap routine and I had to admit the Royal Palace was right when they called them the "World's Greatest." They worked with the mechanical perfection of a smooth-running motor. It was beautiful, but somehow it seemed scarcely human, and the almost-too-perfect precision began to worry me as I watched. And something else worried me; some nameless dread. What was it? Something I had forgotten? I gazed at the dancers, racking my brain for the answer. I knew I had never seen those girls before, yet something about them was familiar to me. And a voice within me kept demanding, "Think! Think! This is important! This is life or death! Think!"

What was it about those dancers, those "Devil's Darlings" that had brought Marjorie so clearly to my mind? God, if only I had guessed then . . .! But I merely sat there, my head an aching void, telling myself that I was simply a grief-stricken fool.

Presently, the dancers streamed into the wings and I watched the following numbers without interest or understanding. However when this was over, the Devil's Darlings made their last appearance—not as dancers, this time, but as nude figures in a tableau that was supposed to represent something in Mythology. Again, I was amazed not only by their beauty, but also by their astonishing similarity. True, there were some slight differences in their faces and in the color of their hair and skin, but if their heads had been covered, their own mothers couldn't have told them apart.

The tableau lasted only a few moments, but it was long enough for me to realize that, this time, that urgent feeling of dread was not clamouring in my brain. I no longer felt the presence of whatever it was that I had noticed in their first appearance.

When the show was over I went backstage with the intention of getting more information about this marvelous troupe of dancers. The doorman knew nothing, but he sent for the theatre's publicity man who turned out to be a chap I'd met several times. His name was Shaw. I told him what I wanted.

He said, "You know just as much about it as I do. They're terrific, aren't they?"

I said, "What do you mean, you don't know anything about them? Where do they come from? Who trained them? Who booked them in here? You must know all that!"

He shook his head. "Feldman—the boss —hired them. And that's all I know. I asked him the same questions you're asking me, but he wouldn't give me a tumble."

"But why? What's Feldman got against publicity?"

"Don't you worry about Feldman." Shaw laughed. "He's smart. I suppose he figures if he can keep 'em a mystery, he'll get more publicity, that way, than he would if everybody knew all about 'em."

"That's possible," I agreed. "But just for my own satisfaction—and with the understanding that I won't print the information—who are they, and where did they come from?"

"The Devil's Darlings? They must have come from hell, I suppose." Then he was serious. "Honestly, Jeff," he said, "I don't know. I've even asked one or two of the girls, myself."

"And they won't say?"

He snorted disgustedly. "Such a bunch of dummies I never saw! Oh, I know you won't believe me—but I'll bet you couldn't get one word out of them."

"I could try," I said.

"No." His reply was slow and somewhat embarrassed. "No, I'm afraid not. For some reason or other, Feldman doesn't want them interviewed. In fact, we've got definite orders not to let any newspaper men backstage. . . . Of course, there's no law to prevent your picking one up, outside."

I took the hint and waited in the street. After awhile, a couple of girls came out. Their coats were of different cut and color, but otherwise, even their faces looked pretty much alike. I stopped them and said, "Girls, I'm reviewing this show for the Times-Tribune and I'd like a few words with you."

They looked at me—as though they were dummies, as Shaw had said—without the slightest expression of intelligence. Puzzled, I went on. "What are your names? Who trained you? Where do you come from? Who is your manager?"

THEY might have been deaf, for all the answer I got. It occurred to me that they think I wasn't on the level. "I'm not trying to pick you up," I told them. "I don't want to take you out to dinner, or buy you a drink, or show you my etchings. I just want a few simple little answers. Now then—" And I started all over again. They turned around and walked away while I was still talking.

Their apparent indifference made me sore and I decided that I wouldn't even mention them in my review. But, though I could keep them out of the paper, I couldn't keep them out of my mind. It was more than mere curiosity . . . it was something about Marjorie — something just beyond the edge of consciousness.

All that night I worried about it, trying to identify the clue that somehow I had missed. The next day, I went back to the Royal Palace, and again the results were the same. During the dance of the Devil's Darlings, I felt that same compelling necessity to answer an unknown question—and again I observed the *absence* of that feeling during the nude tableau.

When the curtain fell, my spirits fell with it, for it seemed I was no nearer to the mystery which I knew in my heart that I must solve. I left the theatre and went to a quiet bar, nearby, where I sat and tried to force my weary brain to think. But, sounding in my aching head like a signal in the ears of a radio operator, went the distracting, staccato rhythm of the dance: "*tap . . . tap . . .tap t'tap-tap. . . . Tap . . . tap . . .*" Over and over, the echo of twenty-four perfectly matched pairs of feet twinkling in intricate and amazing unity. . . .

Suddenly, like a flash of lightning in a cloudless sky, I knew! That dance of the Devil's Darlings was based on a routine that Marjorie had been working on before she disappeared. She had shown it to me one night and had told me how she hoped to sell it to the producer of a musical comedy.

After a moment of breathless speculation, I asked myself: Can this be any more than a strange coincidence? How is it possible for any connection to exist between my wife and these dancers? The dismal probability was simply that someone else had invented the same routine.

Still, I had a gnawing desire to learn more about the Devil's Darlings.

I knew that I would be wasting my time if I tried to question any of those weirdly silent girls again. Instead, I decided to wait until their last performance was over, and then follow one of them to wherever she lived. A few words with a hotel clerk, or housekeeper, or janitor, might be valuable.

I loitered outside the stage door until the girls began to come out. In twos and threes they came, a joyless, subdued group. It seemed significantly strange that nobody met them; they were so beautiful. They turned in different directions, starting, as I supposed for their various homes.

For no better reason than that her hair was the color of Marjorie's, I singled out one of the girls and followed her. I am no expert at shadowing, and if she had been at all suspicious, she would quickly have discovered that I was constantly behind her; but she never glanced around as she led me to Fifth Avenue and Fiftieth Street. Here, she took a bus heading south. At 34th Street, she got off and took a crosstown bus to the Penn Station. Then, much to my surprise, she entered the subway and started back *uptown!* At Fiftieth Street and Broadway, she got out, went up to the street and entered a taxi. I took the next one in the rank and followed her past the point at which we had begun this circular chase, and on to a large, old-fashioned house over by the East River. The girl paid the driver and mounted the stone steps. The door swung open as she approached and closed immediately behind her. There was something sinister about her sudden and silent disappearance.

I dismissed my taxi, and walked up and down the block while I tried to decide on what to do next. Should I simply ring the bell and ask, "Who was the girl who just came in here?" I would probably be thrown out on my neck. Or should I ask for some fictitious person and pretend that I had the wrong address? But before I had come to any decision, two girls passed me under the street light and entered the same door. I recognized them as belonging to the dancing troupe and wondered why, if these three girls had intended to come to the same address, they had not come together.

CHAPTER TWO

The Beauty Treatment

AT LAST I decided to ring the bell and trust to luck. After all, experience on a newspaper gives you plenty of self-confidence in any situation—and besides, what had I to fear?

After a lengthy moment, the door opened and I found myself face to face with a Japanese servant. Without any noticeable accent, he asked, "Yes, sir?"

I looked beyond him at a small, bare hall that contained nothing but a mirror and an ornate table. I said, "I just saw somebody come in here whom I think I know, and I just wanted to—well, to say 'hello.' "

His face was immobile. "And what was the name, sir?"

I made one up. "Parker," I said. "Mary Parker."

"There's no one here by that name, sir." And he started to close the door.

"Wait a second!" I said. "Then who does live here?"

In polite tones, he asked, "Why do you want to know?"

I decided to try another approach. "Look," I said. "Would you like to make a few dollars? Just by answering a question or two?"

With some show of reluctance, he let me step into the hall, after which he closed and locked the heavy door behind me.

"Now then, sir," he said. "What is it you wish?"

I said, "There's something screwy about this troupe called the Devil's Darlings. I'm a reporter—and I want the story."

"The Devil's Darlings?" he repeated as if he had never heard the name before.

"You know what I mean," I insisted. "I just saw three of them come in here. . . . Come on, now—talk. Or . . . shall I find some other way to learn what I want to know?"

I was facing the Jap who was standing in front of the mirror, and as I made that more or less threatening remark, I caught a glimpse in the glass of something moving behind me. Then, as I started to whirl, the world exploded in a shower of blazing lights.

When I returned to aching consciousness, I discovered that I was sitting in a wheel chair, and for a sick moment, I had a flashing vision of myself as a cripple. I tried to move and then I discovered that I was strapped into the chair by leather belts at my arms, legs and waist. The room was small, windowless, and so brightly illuminated that it hurt my eyes. It contained little more in the way of furniture than a massive desk with a chair behind it, and but for me, the room was empty.

In a few seconds, however, the door opened to admit a huge man whose appearance was both startling and somehow fearful. He was tall, heavily built and gave the impression of being the possessor of tremendous physical power. But what caught and held my attention was the man's head—the shock of fiery red hair that was almost like flames licking his skull; the shaggy red eyebrows through which peered eyes of a darker, hotter red; the aquiline nose like the beak of bird of prey; the thin, sharp line of the mouth and the cruel thrust of the jaw. . . .

The man stopped in the doorway and,

much to my astonishment, laughed. "Well!" he said. "Come to, have you? Head ache? Of course it does! Never mind, young man—you'll get rid of that. Along with your head, maybe."

I said, "What the hell does this mean? Take these blasted straps off me—and explain yourself!"

He ignored my demands while he slouched in the chair behind his desk. There was a moment's silence and then he raised his brows to stare at me as if I had been something under a microscope.

"Mr. Ellwood," he said, "I've taken the liberty of examining the papers in your wallet. You know, when you were talking to Koki, my butler, I didn't believe you were a reporter. But now I see I owe you an apology—"

"You owe me a damn sight more than that!" I yelled. "Let me loose, you—"

HE waggled an admonishing finger at me. "That's enough, Mr. Ellwood! Please don't interrupt me again. I don't like it. . . . Now where was I? Oh yes—about your being a reporter. I thought you were a too-inquisitive detective, perhaps—but not a newspaper man. Your reason for being so insistent didn't seem quite adequate—merely that you thought there was something—did you use the word 'screwy?'—about my darlings. Was there, by any chance, some *other* reason for your intrusion here?"

Caution, or antagonism, prompted me to answer, "No. I was only after a story."

"Does the name Marjorie Ellwood mean anything to you?"

My breath caught in my throat, but I managed to shake my head. "No. . . I don't think so. Who is she?"

"Well," he said, "if she had been your wife—or sister—it might have explained your coming here." He nodded sadly. "But now it seems that you are losing your life merely because of your curiosity."

"Losing my *life?*"

"Ah—exactly." Then, slowly, his mouth curved into a hard, mirthless smile and he said, "You know, I've a notion to let you die happy—to satisfy that fatal curiosity of yours. I'll give you the whole, inside story. Of course, you'll never be able to write it. But think how happy you'll be when you go to your death knowing that your last assignment was a success!"

As he finished, he pushed a button on his desk and the door was instantly opened by the Jap, who asked, "Doctor?"

"Just put a strip of tape over Mr. Ellwood's mouth, will you, Koki? I'm going to take him on a tour of inspection, but I think it might be pleasanter without his conversation." He turned to me. "I hope you won't mind, Mr. Ellwood?"

"You dirty—" I began, but before I could get the words out, the Jap had plastered a strip of adhesive across my face. In another second I was unable to make an intelligible sound.

"Koki, you wheel Mr. Ellwood's chair." The doctor stood up. "There's so much to see, I scarcely know where to begin. Perhaps the rehearsal room, first."

With the Jap pushing me and the Mephistophelian doctor striding by my side, we entered a long corridor, like that of a hotel or a hospital.

The doctor said, "I suppose you're surprised at the size of this place? From outside, it looks like a single house, but the fact is that all the houses in this block are connected—which gives us quite a large establishment . . . dormitories, rehearsal rooms, hospital, infirmary, punishment cells, gymnasium. And, oh—play rooms, of course. We're just passing one of the play rooms, now. Shall we glance in for a moment?"

The doctor stopped, opened a door, and suddenly the air was filled with clamor of screams and coarse laughter. Koki swung my chair about and shoved it through the door.

It was like a scene from some luxurious and orgiastic hell—a hideous mingling of pain and wealth. The room, itself, was hung and carpetted in rich, black velvet. The only furniture was a number of low couches and on these lolled perhaps six or seven men in evening dress. So intent were they in watching the spectacle in the middle of the floor that they scarcely glanced up at us as we made our entrance.

In the center of the floor two girls were fighting with whips. They were nearly nude and each had her left arm tied behind her so that no protection could be offered to any blow. As I watched, one of them slashed the other across the breasts with such ferocious savagery that the blood spurted from the tender skin. . . . They fought until they fell. And then they were dragged to their feet and the senseless fight recommenced; blow after blow.

A T MY side, the doctor laughed. "It's an amusing game," he said. "Are you wondering why those girls are willing to fight? It's so simple. The one who loses will get something so much worse, that she'll wish she were still fighting. . . . But let us go on."

Again we were in the corridor with the door to that ghastly "playroom" closed behind us. Only one thought was in my brain: *Marjorie!* Where in this mad tenement of torment was she? What had they done to her? Was she still alive? I almost hoped not. And desperately, meanwhile, I strained against the straps that bound me, but there was not the slightest indication of loosening, anywhere. Total paralysis could not have made me more completely helpless.

Presently, we entered a much larger room—obviously the rehearsal hall, for at one end of it, a double line of girls were practicing a dance step to music supplied by a phonograph. But for high heeled slippers and some sort of abbreviated garment which they wore around their waists, the chorus was completely unclothed. Several men in white uniforms were sitting on a bench along the side of the room and I noticed that each clutched the stock of a short whip in his right hand.

From the farther end of the hall, a woman's voice cried, "No, no! Not like that, girls!" Abruptly, the music ceased, and Marjorie—my own Marjorie—pressed through the lines of the chorus, turned about and faced them. Thus, her bare back was presented to us and even from that distance I could see the red brands of pain that the whips had crisscrossed on her flesh.

"Now watch me again! Music! . . . One, two . . ."

The doctor was speaking. "It was fortunate that we were able to obtain the young lady's services. She is an excellent dance director. And by the way, you should be interested in her because her name is—"

At that moment, Marjorie crumpled to her knees, moaning, "I can't do any more, I tell you! . . . I can't! . . . I'm too tired."

Casually, one of the white uniformed men rose from the bench and sauntered over to Marjorie where she lay sobbing on the floor. He raised his whip, brought it down and it was as if he had struck me on the naked heart. He raised the whip again, but its biting descent was arrested in mid-air at the doctor's command.

"Wait a second! Bring her here!"

Obediently, the man dragged her to her feet and forced her to walk toward us. As she approached, her tear-stained, frightened eyes were fixed on the doctor's face.

The doctor said, "Young lady, I'm inclined to think you have outlived your usefulness as a dance director. . . . And I'm afraid you're not quite young enough to join the chorus, yourself . . . so perhaps we'll try you in South America." The gaze of his red eyes fell to Marjorie's breasts, so ill-concealed by a silken bandeau, and he added significantly, "After a few little alterations . . ."

"Please!" Marjorie gasped. "Please! Not that!"

The doctor laughed and asked, "May I present a name-sake of yours? Mr. Ellwood—"

For the first time, her eyes met mine. I saw the sudden gleam of hope and recognition in her eyes, and the instant reaction of bottomless despair. "Jeff!" she sobbed, "Oh, darling—they've got you, too—"

Then she fainted and her guard let her slip to the floor.

"Well, well," said the doctor, "so you wanted more, here, than just a story, didn't you? Well, that makes it more interesting for both of us. I'll know that you won't be bored as I show you the rest of the establishment. How could you be, when your wife is so—involved with it?" Then, to the guard, he said, "Take her to the surgery!"

A T THE doctor's direction, Koki wheeled my chair around and as we left the rehearsal room, I glimpsed my wife's unconscious body being carried toward another exit, past the lines of motionless and apparently incurious dancers.

As we started down the corridor the doctor paused and exclaimed, "How inconsiderate of me! There's no necessity for keeping that adhesive plaster over your mouth as long as you know that anything rude or insulting you say to me would have a serious effect on your wife's comfort. . . . Koki—strip off the bandage!"

The Jap ripped off the adhesive tape, and then I realized that I was safer gagged—or at least that Marjorie was safer. Curses rose in my throat like something solid that would choke me, but I knew how futile and how dangerous they were. A voice within me warned that if ever I was to save Marjorie from the last horror of this place, it would be by guile, and not by threats.

"There!" said the doctor. "Is that better?"

"Much better, thank you." (Nothing was ever so difficult as trying to be civil to that red devil.)

"Good!" he said. "Now, if there are any questions you want to ask, don't hesitate to ask them. Since you'll never be able to use the information, I'll be delighted to tell you anything you want to know."

"There are a lot of things I want to know," I told him. "So many that I hardly know what to ask first. . . Where do you get so many girls who look almost exactly alike? Why, you couldn't do that if you were trying to cast a legitimate show on Broadway! And how are you able to let them out of this place and be sure they won't go straight to the police? And—"

He interrupted me with a laugh. "One at a time, Mr. Ellwood! But here we are at the gymnasium. I can answer at least part of one of your questions here. . ."

The "gymnasium" was not like any other in the world. At first glance, it was more like a factory, for it was filled with large pieces of machinery which were unlike any I had ever seen. For instance, there was one contrivance that seemed to consist of nothing more than a great number of rubber balls held together by a network of springs; another seemed to be a giant electrical vibrator; a third one resembled the iron lung used in the treatment for infantile paralysis. At one side, was a separate glass cabinet about ten feet square and it was to this spot that Koki directed my chair.

Within the brightly lit cabinet were three persons: two men who were stripped to the waist, and a young woman in the center, suspended by her wrists from a scaffolding. With unmerciful strength, the men were pounding the girl's hips and thighs with heavy rubber paddles. I could see that she was screaming, but little of the sound emerged.

"I told you I'd answer part of one of your questions," said the doctor. "What you're watching now is a young lady who is literally being beaten into shape. You see, it makes very little difference to me whether I get good 'raw material' to start with. Let them be fat or thin—as ugly as you please—I'll turn out beauties in the end—and as alike as two peas in a pod. . . . This reducing cabinet is really very efficient—it's about one hundred and twenty-five degrees in there. The heat, together with the beating, takes fat off with surprising speed. Then, some of these other inventions of mine provide the finishing touches, so far as the legs, hips and arms are concerned. . ."

I asked, "But why is it necessary to inflict so much pain in the process? Surely it's not—"

"But it *is* necessary!" he cut in. "Don't you see why?"

"No."

"You will," he promised. "You will. . . . Come! We're keeping Mrs. Ellwood waiting!"

CHAPTER THREE

Horror's Pattern

IN the surgery, Marjorie was strapped to an operating table, a man in a white apron standing beside her. I had hoped that she would still be unconscious, but her eyes were open and filled with such mortal terror that I could not restrain the groan that rose within me.

Warningly, the doctor cautioned, "Remember, Mr. Ellwood— If you love your wife—" Then he turned to his assistant and asked, "Ready?"

"Yes, Doctor."

As he drew on a pair of rubber gloves, the doctor said, "You were wondering how it happens that my girls are so similar in body and face. Plastic surgery is the simple answer. An ugly nose, eyes that are too small, an unpleasant chin line —all are easily corrected. Even easier, is a case like that of your wife whose defect is merely that her breasts are somewhat too large." He chose a scalpel from the instrument table and moved to Marjorie's side.

"For God's sake!" I cried, "Aren't you going to give her an anaesthetic?"

"Certainly not!"

Ignoring my wife's shrieks of agony, the doctor began the operation by cutting a long incision at the lower juncture of the breast and the torso. Then, two small circles were cut—one at the edge of the areola, and the other, of the same size, a couple of inches above it. After this, the skin was pulled away from the quivering flesh beneath it, and the actual work of remodelling was begun. . . . How long it was before the last stitch was taken, I have no idea, but when, at last, the operating table was wheeled out of the room, I realized that my clothes were soaking with perspiration and that a trickle of blood was running down my chin from my lacerated lip.

"That's done!" said the doctor, stripping off his gloves. "And a good job, too. In a week or so, she'll be well again—and more beautiful than she ever was before. In South America, she should be very, very successful." He smiled at the thought and motioned to Koki to turn my chair about. Then he said, "I'm afraid I have several little duties to perform, now, so if you don't mind, I think I'll put you away until tomorrow. . . . Down to the cellar, Koki!"

I asked, "Then you're not going to kill me, tonight?"

"Tonight? Oh dear, no! You surely

don't think I'd deprive you of the pleasure of attending your wife's—shall we say, coming out party? We'll give her quite a reception, here, before she sails for Rio. I'm sure you wouldn't want to miss it. After that, of course. . ."

By means of an elevator, we descended to the cellar and started down a narrow, concrete passageway. The floor, I noticed, was damp, but little did I guess how fortunate for me that fact was to become. . . . As we passed one of the row of doors which were deeply recessed in the stone wall, we heard a woman moaning as if in delirium. The doctor stopped and opened the door with a key.

Against the wall of the cell was a young woman who was held erect by ropes which bound her wrists and ankles. Perhaps a hundred tiny pins had been stuck into her body. From the head of each pin ran a thin wire to some sort of an electrical machine at her feet.

The doctor said, "I take some pride in this invention. As you can see, those pins are so small that they don't do any damage worth mentioning and, just by themselves, they wouldn't even hurt very much. But with the addition of an electric shock, it's a different matter! Look at the muscles ripple under her skin as first one group of pins and then another delivers the charge!"

BUT I was looking at the small blue heart tattooed on her arm. That this beautiful creature could be the same, blousy burlesque queen whose picture I had seen, seemed impossible; yet there could be no doubt that it was she.

I asked, "What could she have done to deserve such terrible treatment?"

"Terrible?" The doctor raised his satanic eyebrows. "This isn't terrible! Why, if I put her to bed, now, she'd be well tomorrow morning. It's painful, I agree— but it's not doing any real injury." And he added, *"Except to her brain!"*

"Do you mean that she'll go mad?"

He shook his head. "Not entirely. But a certain amount of pain breaks down resistance to—er—suggestion. You've probably noticed it yourself, at some time or other. Take a person who is really suffering, even if it's only a toothache; tell him to *do* something, anything, even though it's the last thing in the world he wants to do. Still, he'll do it. His own will is temporarily weak. But only temporarily. If pain is much more violent and prolonged, the will does not entirely return when the patient recovers, and with each treatment, the individual's will becomes weaker until finally, he, or she, becomes an ideal subject for the most elementary hypnosis."

So that was the doctor's inhuman theory! And that explained why he had operated upon Marjorie without anaesthetic: to weaken her mind to such a point that she would be willing to do his bidding without question or revolt. I understood all too clearly that if the suffering she had already undergone was not sufficient, she would be subjected to more.

We left the poor girl's cell and her constant moaning dimmed as we went along the passageway. The doctor threw open a door and Koki wheeled me into a bare, stone room which contained nothing more than a cot. Then the doctor took a gun out of his pocket and stood in the doorway.

To Koki, he said, "Take the straps off him!" And to me, "Please don't try anything heroic, Mr. Ellwood. It would be quite useless—and I should hate to lose you so early."

I stood up stiffly. Koki wheeled the chair out into the passage. As the doctor backed out after him, he said, "And now —good night!"

Now, I'm not going to give you a full account of the week that followed. Instead, I'm going to try to tell only the essentials, partly because I, myself, would like to forget some of the things I saw. . . . The night when the girl with the tattooed heart surrendered to a group of men who used her as a target in the game of darts; the 'Roman Carnival' that was staged in one of the larger playrooms; the treatment of a girl who was scarcely more than a child, yet who had been given a woman's form by the doctor's devilish art. . . .

No—I would not think of that. I'll tell you, instead, about my cell. As I have said, it contained nothing but a cot. From the first moment when I was left alone, I tried to scheme some means of escape, but there was no window. The walls were as solid as the side of a mountain and whenever the heavy wooden door was opened, the doctor was there with a gun in his hand. I think it was on the fourth day that I first realized the possible value of a heavily shielded electric cable that ran along the base of one wall. Doubtless, it was the main power line—and this house used a great deal of power. Anyhow, without a plan clearly in my mind, I began to strip the insulation from the wire. I knew that it was dangerous because the floor was damp and the slightest contact with the bare copper would send me into instant oblivion.

UNLESS you've tried to strip a heavy cable without pliers or knife—with only your fingernails for tools—you don't know how tough the covering is. It took two nights of constant labor to dispose of the outer layers of fabric and rubber over a length of possibly four inches. However, while I worked, I planned. My scheme was mad, perhaps—with the madness of desperation—but it was the only chance I had. I waited until the seventh day to take the springs of the cot apart. They were not coil springs, thank God, but the long kind that run from the head to the foot of the frame. Attached together, end to end, three of them were

enough to lead from the break in the insulation of the cable to the iron handle of the door. I fixed the wire spring around the door handle and left the other end free, winding it close to the end with the two blankets that had been given me. Then, holding the blanket-wound spring in my hand, I sat down beside the power line to wait. . . .

The hours dragged heartbreakingly. . . . I had not been allowed to see Marjorie again, but the doctor had taken a sadistic pleasure in reporting her progress and had boasted of the speed of her recovery and of the perfection of the work he had done. And what he called her "coming-out party" was to be tonight. After a time, a terrible fear clutched me. Had I been forgotten? Would they lead Marjorie to her ordeal without having me there as a helpless witness?

At last I heard footsteps in the passageway! My heart leaped painfully and my hands were trembling as I grasped the spring through its blanket covering. Then came the sound of the key in the lock . . . the turning handle . . . the slowly opening door—and I jammed the bare end of the spring against the exposed copper of the power line!

Koki uttered no sound, but stood there with the iron handle in his hand. For a ghastly moment, I thought that I had failed, but then I saw how stiff he was—held, absolutely motionless by the deadly current that was crashing through his body.

Unaware of what had happened, the doctor stood in the lighted passage. "Come, Mr. Ellwood!" he said. "The party has already begun. I'm sure your wife will be hurt if you're not there to see her debut. . . . What's the matter, Koki? Go on!" And he put his hand on the Jap's shoulder as if to push him. That was the end of him—and I only wish to God that his death had not been so quick and easy.

JUST to be certain, I held the spring and power line in contact for several minutes before I separated them. There was a smell of burning fat in the cell. When I disconnected the spring, Koki and the doctor slumped to the floor as their dead muscles suddenly relaxed.

Both men carried guns. Putting them in the side pockets of my coat, I raced along the passage, up the stairs to the first floor corridor, down the deserted corridor to the playroom where the doctor had told me the party would be given. Cautiously, I opened the door and slipped inside— but my caution was unnecessary, for nobody looked up.

About twenty men were sitting in easy chairs that were arranged around a circular platform. Most of the men were old, and some of them even decrepit, but all were dressed in faultless evening clothes. At the base of the platform, four uniformed guards faced the octogenarian audience.

When I entered, the room was in partial darkness, but as I concealed myself behind a section of the wall draperies, a soft spotlight came to a focus on the top of the bare platform. Then, a man arose from the audience and, as he began to speak, I recognized him. It was Feldman, of the Royal Palace Theatre.

"Gentlemen," he said, "now that we have disposed of our preliminary attractions, it gives us great pleasure to present a young lady who is destined to delight our South American friends. However, we felt it would be a shame to let her go without giving her an opportunity to enjoy our own hospitality. . ."

Slowly rising from the center of the platform was a huge wooden cross and, hanging to it, the glorious body of my wife—like a statue of unblemished marble. Instead of nails, or ropes, her wrists and ankles were tied with velvet ribbons. When the entire cross had emerged, it began to turn—the better to display her.

A longdrawn sigh swept over the audience and Feldman's voice continued. "To introduce her this way—on a cross— is merely a symbol . . . a symbol of her willingness to sacrifice anything for your pleasure. . . ."

At that instant, Feldman moved so that he faced me directly. I got him through the stomach. I killed two of the guards before they had a chance to draw, and a third fired one shot before his brains splattered among the fleeing, panic stricken men. The fourth guard got away in the crowd without attempting any defense. In not more than fifteen seconds, the place was empty save but for Marjorie and me. . . .

Even after all these weeks, Marjorie is not quite—well, "sane" isn't the word. It's hard to explain, but she's like an obedient child. Physically, she's as perfect as any woman alive; but mentally? She'll do anything she's told, without question or argument—anything. . . . Naturally, I keep track of her every moment of the day and night. I only hope the doctors are right in assuring me that, in time, she will be normal, again.

Of course, Feldman's scheme was to *create* beauty and to capitalize on it in every possible way and, with the doctor's skilled assistance, he was well on the road to success. I hope their souls are rotting in the hell they deserve!

One thing worries me above all else. The doctor (whose true name I never learned) told me that he accomplished his results by means of pain *and hypnosis*. Now, he is dead. Is it vain to hope that time, alone, will some day remove the spell he cast?

THE END

HOUSE OF HORRIBLE LAUGHTER

By RAY CUMMINGS   *(Author of "Death's Dreadful Lover," etc.)*

We were safe, Bob and I, as long as we trembled at the horrors we witnessed in that house. It was only after we felt a strange, evil thrill coursing in our blood at the sight of those fiendishly tortured girls, that our feet began slipping over the brink of the Black Pit. . . .

BOB didn't want me to go. The fact that for three months I had been trying to get on the professional stage with no luck at all, and that this looked like my big chance, made no difference to him.

"Look here, Anne," he protested, "if Stanley Tarrington wants to try you out for a job, let him do it at his office. He didn't have to invite you to his home—at night."

We had an argument; it ended by Bob insisting that he would go with me. We started in his little car, about eight o'clock that evening—the appointment was for

nine-thirty, at Tarrington's country estate, in New Jersey. It was a drizzling, foggy summer night. Bob drove fast; we found ourselves presently winding up through lonely hills, sodden in the mist-dank fields; by scattered farmhouses, and on the hillcrests, the lights of occasional summer residences. I had never been here; had seen Stanley Tarrington only once.

Bob, who is a feature writer for the New York *Comet,* knew Tarrington by reputation, though he had never met him. He had reviewed one of the Tarrington productions a year or so ago. He told me now that he didn't like Tarrington, his theatrical methods, nor his shows. I wasn't impressed; it seemed to me that Bob was prejudiced because he was in love with me—abnormally sensitive for my welfare.

To me, being connected with Stanley Tarrington was a golden opportunity. In the world of the theatre Tarrington was well known. Up to a year ago he had produced many musical shows. With business as well as artistic genius he was said to have amassed a fortune. Then suddenly he had retired. Ill-health, I understood, so that he had isolated himself in this country home.

A WEEK ago I had seen an unobtrusive little ad. He was seeking girls for some new musical venture. I had found what seemed a temporary office, with a crowd of show-girls whom he was interviewing in person. My turn came at last; and I stood before him in his private room, with my heart pounding.

"Anne Gloster, you say?"

"Yes, Mr. Tarrington."

"Age?"

"Seventeen. I'll be eighteen next month."

He sat with his appraising gaze roving me. I saw him as a big, heavy-set man of indeterminate age—a heavy face, with a small, very black mustache, contrasting with his greying bushy brows and grey-black hair close-cropped on a bullet head. I should have been warned by the gleam in his eyes, the half-smile of approval that twitched at his thin bluish lips, because assuredly I am no fool. I had to tell him that I had never been on the professional stage, and had merely amateur training in singing and dancing. Certainly his swift interest in me should have seemed queer; but at the time it only thrilled me with excitement.

"You live with your parents?" he said.

"No. I'm an orphan. My relatives are all in Kansas. I live alone. I've got to support myself—" I smiled frankly— "I've only been in the city three months and my money's about gone."

"You—look all right," he said after another long silence. I recall now that the words came with a very queer sucking of his breath. His big thick hands seemed to tense on the arms of his chair, with whitening knuckles as his gaze still roved over me.

I am, I think, rather a distinctive type —small and very dark, with what Bob calls a vivid Spanish beauty. I cannot use much cosmetics—I'm vivid enough. Bob says I make him dizzy when I turn my eyes on him. He says they promise too much. Heavens knows, I don't mean it— certainly not for anyone but Bob. . . .

Tarrington's gaze was down at my feet. "The figure is important," he said slowly. "The legs—" At his gesture I raised my skirt a few inches and he laughed.

"That is all right, Miss Gloster—I do not want to startle you." He stood up, towering beside me. He seemed to sway; his hands came up, and for an instant I thought they were reaching for my shoulders. But he backed away and stood rocking on his heels, as he made the appointment for my tryout. . . .

I told Bob none of these details. We were at this time, approximately engaged, with nothing standing between us but lack of money, which made me all the more determined to earn something substantial.

"That could be the place," Bob said out of a long silence.

You couldn't see much in the drizzling fog—a dank, rolling, empty countryside, with a cluster of lights on top of a hill. Then we turned into a gateway, with a sign Tarrington Manor. We climbed the hill, and pulled up under the porte cochere of what seemed a tremendous rambling frame mansion.

"Quite a rehearsal," Bob muttered sardonically as we climbed out. "See all the crowd, Anne?"

I must confess I was already glad that Bob was with me. There were no cars here; no sign of life, save the yellow rectangles of the brocaded windows which shifted their light out into the dreary fog; no sound except the wind in the trees and the sodden drip of the rain from the building cornices.

We thumped the knocker at a big oaken door. It opened presently; swung inward to disclose a dim foyer, with a giant Negro standing to one side. I gasped; I felt Bob's hand on my arm; and, far from entering, we recoiled a step and stood staring. The Negro was well over six feet; his hips were bound with a black loin cloth; his muscular black body glistened in the yellow-red sheen of a big iron lamp which hung in the entryway—smooth ebony skin shining as though oiled. He took a step toward us and gestured; the muscles of his magnificent body rippled under his skin. He suggested a huge eunuch guarding the door of the harem of some Oriental potentate. . . .

"Miss Gloster?" he said. "Come in."

THEN I think he saw Bob for the first time. A look of startled indecision swept him.

Bob said briskly, "Is Mr. Tarrington here?"

"Yes," said the Negro. "Miss Gloster has an appointment."

He stood as though to exclude Bob . . . In just that instant there was so strong a premonition of menace flooding me that I almost turned to draw Bob back to our car . . . If only I had done it—spared us this horror which even now makes me shudder at its memory.

Bob said, "Tell Mr. Tarrington we'll wait here—we'd like to see him please."

Good old Bob—he knew what it meant to me to get into a Tarrington produc-

tion; and despite his misgivings, he felt I was in no danger with him beside me.

The Negro gestured again. "You wait in the reception room. He will come."

My heart was racing unnaturally. We went through the doorway. Threshold of horror. I felt it then as surely as though these draped walls, this hot, incense-laden air, were screaming it at me.

The giant black led us perhaps twenty feet along a broad dim corridor, stalking in advance of us with his bare feet padding on the mahogany floor. Again I had the feeling that a eunuch was showing us into his master's harem. The corridor was glowing with a dim red sheen. There was nothing to be seen save draped walls. Then we passed a recess where under a faint glow of pallid violet light stood the life-size statue of a nude woman. Palms and potted flowers half shrouded her—a figure of pink-white marble, with the pale light glistening on her like moonlight . . . The thing was so realistic that for a second I thought it was a living woman posing there.

The reception room was small, somberly draped, dimly lighted. There was a couch piled with velour pillows; a big brass samovar in the corner, with a brass tea-tray before it; and a few easy chairs.

"Sit down," the Negro said. "Mr. Tarrington will come in a moment."

We sat staring at each other as he stalked out.

"Well," Bob murmured, when the footsteps had died away, "if there's going to be a theatrical rehearsal here tonight, that fellow is already dressed for some kind of part."

Some such vague idea had occurred to me; but in my heart I knew there was something of menace here—something horrible. And Bob felt it, though he grinned now at me while we sat expectantly listening to the silence of the house. Heavy unnatural silence. I felt suddenly as though it were a silence pregnant with sound; as though all this strange exotic interior were draped and padded to muffle its activities. What activities? The very question itself seemed to mask something horrible.

And I was conscious that my heart still was pounding. The air was hot, heavy with incense; I could feel perspiration breaking out all over me . . . Two or three minutes passed. Bob had gotten up and was standing by the table where a big glass-bowled Turkish pipe stood with a litter of magazines around it. He picked up some of the magazines, glancing at them by the glow of the table lamp . . . *Caras y Caretas . . . La Vie Parisienne.*

"Well," he murmured, "this bird Tarrington seems to have gay ideas. . . . Better loosen your wrap, Anne—it's damnably hot in here."

I gestured and he stooped over me. I whispered, "If—if he doesn't come in a minute, let's get out of here. I—feel queer—"

He stared. I saw that his face was flushed by heat, with beads of sweat on his forehead.

"Right," he agreed. "Whatever you say. There's certainly something very—"

He stopped, startled. We both tensely listened. From out in the corridor came the sound of a girl's laughter. There was a patter of footsteps—running, dancing tread, and the throbbing voice of a girl singing.

BOB had gone to the doorway and I ran and joined him. Fifty feet away there was a cross corridor. We had a brief glimpse of a girl half running, half dancing. Then another followed her—young girls perhaps no older than I. Their white limbs weaved in brief billowing black gauze drapes; their hair was flowing free.

Performers gaily on their way to a rehearsal here? If it had seemed that, Bob

and I could have peered with interest. But at the corridor crossing one of them suddenly tripped and fell. Her song went into an eerie throbbing sob; and as the other stooped to pick her up they stood clinging together, swaying, then laughing. Maudlin? It could have been that. They were gone past our sight in a moment, staggering and laughing, pawing at each other. It seemed that one was ripping off the other's drapery. . . . Then their raucous shouts were mingled with the angry muttering voice of the Negro. . . .

What weird horror was this of which we had had so unexpected a glimpse? The gayety of the girls—something about it made us both shudder. Bob was gripping my arm. "Come on," he murmured. "Let's get out of here."

"Oh, good evening, Miss Gloster."

From a doorway which we had not noticed, Stanley Tarrington suddenly was in the corridor confronting us.

"Good evening," I gasped. "Are—are we late? My friend, Mr. Rance, came with me."

"Miss Gloster's fiancé," Bob said grimly. "I understand you're having professional tryouts here tonight, Mr. Tarrington?"

Tarrington was dressed very much as he had been in his office. He bowed a little, smiling imperturbably at Bob.

"Yes. That is so. I have my own private auditorium here—I find I can judge performers better, here in the quiet relaxation of my home."

"Oh," Bob said. "And you think that Miss Gloster—"

I noticed that Tarrington was staring at Bob intently. And suddenly he broke in:

"Did you say your name was Rance?"

"Yes," Bob said. "Miss Gloster—"

"Robert Rance? Of the *Comet* by any chance?"

Why did I not have the wit to interpret that dark smouldering glance! It roved Bob musingly.

"The *Comet*," Bob said. "Correct. I'm in the dramatic department."

Tarrington's face showed a vague sr''e. "Ah yes—I seem to remember—"

It meant nothing to Bob. His mind was all on me. His gesture waved away the topic. He said,

"You're interested possibly in employing Miss Gloster?"

Tarrington seemed to come out of his roving thoughts with a jerk. "I am casting an original production—" His gaze went to me and clung. His breath went out with his words, as it had in his office when he stared like this at me. Then he suddenly turned back to Bob.

"I think I have a part for Miss Gloster," he said crisply. "We shall see . . . Would you care to come and watch, Mr. Rance?"

"Thanks," Bob said.

THE offer, the crisp businesslike tone, for that moment reassured us both. We followed him past the cross corridor —there was no one in sight down its dim lengths. Doorways were closed. The heavy silence again seemed brooding over everything. We passed a dimly lighted room. It was crowded with Oriental trophies—I recalled that Stanley Tarrington in former years was said to have traveled extensively. . . . We went through a small art gallery . . . Gorgeous nudes in ornate gold frames . . . I saw a Henner—drooping girl figure, titian haired, hips blue draped; blue sky, blue water of the pool beside which the girl was sitting . . . And the Goya nude Duchess, white and voluptuous upon her black velvet couch. . . .

"I am giving a little tryout performance," Tarrington said back over his shoulder as we followed him through the gallery and into another corridor. "I think it would be well for Miss Gloster to watch it for a time—then I will put her in it."

We were passing along an almost dark patch of hallway. There seemed a pant to Tarrington's voice, as though his breath were labored. And I was aware again of my pounding heart; my breath sucking in and out through parted lips as I clung to Bob's arm with Tarrington in advance of us. And as though reading my thoughts, Bob suddenly stooped and whispered,

"This fool incense—damned queer—"

Incense? Certainly the air was redolent with an exotic perfume. It had met us at the front door, and was growing stronger now as we advanced into the enormous rambling interior. But there was something more than perfume, a humid breathless heat, that was making us pant. Some queer quality to the air itself. I sensed it now for the first time . . . And as I nodded to Bob, and squeezed his arm, suddenly I heard myself laughing softly. There was something thrilling about the feel of my sweat-bathed limbs; evaporation made them tingle with coolness as I walked . . . My face felt hot and flushed; with every breath there was coming to me now a queer lightness —an exhilaration . . . Soon I would be dancing for Tarrington—the great producer . . . My big chance . . . Fame . . . Money. Bob and I could get married . . . I squeezed his arm . . . I'd show Tarrington that I could dance . . . with the impeding clothes cast away— never in my life had I felt that I could dance better than now. . . .

"Anne—what the devil?"

I must have been chuckling to myself. At Bob's startled murmur, I whispered, "I'm all right. Isn't it—exciting. I'll show him how good I am—you'll see."

But under it all, as though I were intoxicated and knew it, that same apprehension of horror was persisting; as though now I were being swept along—helpless—laughing, but frightened. . . .

House of horrible happiness . . . Like hysteria—one may laugh and cry. . . . I could laugh in this weird place; laugh—and scream with terror. . . .

"This way if you please," Tarrington said. He opened a blank, black door. It clicked behind us. Bob muttered with a startled exclamation as we found ourselves almost in darkness—a small, black-walled room, with a big rectangular plate glass panel. A couch was before it. There seemed nothing else in the room.

"Sit down," Tarrington said.

The glass pane overlooked a glowingly lighted apartment, which was at a lower level some ten feet beneath us. It was like looking through an observation window down into a broadcasting studio. . . .

"You will sit here," Tarrington said. His hand on my arm drew me to the couch. I sucked in my breath as he seated me, with Bob beside me.

"My little performance will start in a moment," Tarrington added softly. "You will like to watch it—from here. It is amusing." He laughed vaguely. "Then I will call you down—"

"If she decides she wants the job," Bob said.

"Yes—of course—if I decide I want her," Tarrington retorted. "Aren't you too warm, Miss Gloster? Give me your wrap."

He whisked it from my shoulders. "Thanks," I said. "Will I—will I dance in costume?"

"Yes—perhaps." He moved away; the door clicked and he was gone.

A LOW music was throbbing from somewhere now and we sat silent, staring down through the glass panel. It

was a square wooden apartment. The windows and doors were solidly draped in black. The ceiling, some twenty feet above the level of our window, was shrouded in black velour—a simulated sky in which tiny stars were twinkling.

The floor was artificial grass—banks of sward, with vivid artificial flowers and plants—an exotic tropic garden, pallid with a light like moonlight from some hidden source. An ancient garden. Steps between small marble columns, led down to a small pool whose water rippled in the light of burning braziers from which a faint blue smoke was rising. . . .

I felt Bob shift uneasily beside me; saw him vaguely as he turned his head, furtively gazing at the darkness of the blank little room in which we were sitting. Then his hand came to my lap, found my hand and clutched it; his fingers were cold and dank.

But the scene through the panel held me, so that I sat peering. Empty, pallid garden, throbbing with music. Were there no actors? Abruptly there was movement down in the little glowing garden. From the floor by the walls, a score of panels slid up—ten foot mirrors standing now amid the flowers and palms. The garden broadened, with the duplicated scene; it was as though each mirror opened a vista through a flowered recess to new distances of the erotic garden. . . .

Then Bob muttered, "There's Tarrington—"

The thick stalwart figure of Tarrington came striding into the scene. His coat was off, his shirtsleeves rolled, baring muscular forearms matted with black hair. In his hand he brandished a foot-long metal cylinder, a sort of handle from which hung a white wire nearly the length of his body. He came through a doorway, advancing over the green sward with vigorous striding step. Alone in the scene, he stopped before a mirror, surveying himself. Then he tentatively swung the cylinder; the wire lashed through the air with a snapping whizz.

"What the devil—" Bob muttered.

Was Tarrington to be, not Director here, but an actor so that now he must survey himself to gauge his aspect? Again the wire lashed with its whining whizz, snapping at the end of its arc as dexterously Tarrington flicked it back. Then he stooped, picked up a long black cord from the floor, and attached it to the bottom of his cylinder-handle. The cord slithered behind him like a great black snake as he walked.

Queer . . . But my attention was whirled from it. Tarrington had come closer to us. The light struck more squarely upon his face. An actor here? It seemed so, for we saw now that his face was altered by make-up—his nose broadened, with bridge raised hawk-like. The line of his eyebrows was changed; his hair now was greased and slicked back from his retreating forehead.

I felt myself shuddering. It was as though, by this art of the theatre, he had revealed his true self. The suave theatrical magnate was gone. Here was a figure of brutal, vicious cunning, animal-like with leashed ferocity.

Then suddenly he raised a hand and called over the throbbing music.

"Ready, Zaro?"

"Yes, Master."

We saw at one end of the room a giant Negro, clad in trousers and shirt.

"Lights! Camera!" Tarrington added.

WHITE Kleig lights sprang with focused beams upon the area at the end of the pool where Tarrington was standing. And we saw the Negro pulling aside a drape. A huge modern motion picture camera was revealed. The Negro rolled its big tripod forward, stood adjusting it. . . .

A motion picture studio! . . . I heard Bob mutter it as breathlessly we stared . . . A silent picture. We saw no sound apparatus. And Tarrington now called,

"Ready, Nina? Entrance! . . ."

The camera was clicking. From the draped room-wall, beyond its angle of vision, three girls in dark veils came gliding. I stiffened. What ghastly realism was this? The girls were pushing a wheeled tripod upon which an eight-foot wooden cross was mounted. A man was lashed with chains to the cross—a big man with a mop of iron-gray hair. He was in shirt and trousers—ragged garments, red with the crimson of his blood.

Then Bob was bending down over me, his voice at my ear:

"That Negro—guarding us—"

I heard myself murmuring, "Bob— Good God—"

Negro? The Negro was down there operating the motion picture camera. But I saw now that he was not the one who had admitted us to this ghastly place, for as I followed Bob's gaze I dimly could see the other giant black form standing here in the cubby behind us, arms folded upon the brawny naked chest as he silently stood watching.

"We're trapped," Bob murmured.

It swept me with a rush of terror, and the dim reflected light through the glass panel showed Bob's face, white and grim.

"I'll try and get us out," he whispered. "If only I had a gun—or if I can get him to leave us for a minute—"

"Yes—" I gasped.

"We'll make a run for it," Bob added. "Good Lord, look at them down there—"

Despite our own terror the horrible scene below held us fascinated . . . The camera was steadily clicking. The music was throbbing with a wild barbaric rhythm . . . The dancing girls, waving the dark veils around their pallid bodies, were encircling the crucified man on the cross. And Tarrington stood confronting the victim.

Monstrous tableau which the camera now was recording. The crucified man sagged limp, sodden with his blood. And Tarrington stood before him, snarling with bared teeth so that suddenly all vestige of human aspect left his face.

"You're conscious, Blakely?"

The man on the cross seemed trying to lift his sagging head. And suddenly one of the girls dancing past laughed wildly. Horrible broken laughter with a sob of terror in it. The others clutched at her as she swayed.

It made Tarrington whirl. His wire lash flicked out—caught the girl's veil with dexterous skill and tore it from her.

"Master—have mercy—" She half screamed it with sobbing terror, and her two companions cast her off.

"Master—have mercy—"

The snapping crack of the wire split her words as the demoniac Tarrington lashed it upon her shrinking white body. And then he laughed and backed away.

"You know your part, Nina. . . . Make no more errors—"

She had half fallen and her shuddering companions picked her up. And one of them gasped,

"She's—all right now. She won't do it again, Master. But we—we want more air. You know how we need it—"

"You're having enough," Tarrington rasped. "You'll have more soon. Dance now—this is the torture scene—the camera is on us—"

Ghastly realism . . . the torture scene . . . "More air—you know how we need it . . ." What could that mean? . . . What monstrous mystery was this? . . . Numbed, blurred thoughts swept me in those horrible seconds. . . .

AGAIN Tarrington was fronting the crucified man. "So you still are conscious, Blakely?"

"Yes—" It was a low gasp, quivering with physical agony. "Haven't you done enough to me, Tarrington?"

"Enough? Why that was rehearsal. We come now to the real torture scene. The camera is on us. It will make a wonderful picture for my South American and Oriental markets . . . You don't like my theatrical methods, do you Blakely?"

"You—you damnable—"

"Realist, Blakely. I go in for realism. You broke me in the American theatre—you with your damned influence to have me blacklisted? You thought I'd retire? Oh no! Merely shifted my activities. My motion pictures are very realistic. My foreign markets are eager for them. You found that out too, didn't you—with your damnable snooping detective work? In another week you'd have exposed me again. . . ."

Demoniac vengeful triumph was in Tarrington's voice. "But now I've got you, Blakely. You—Czar of the ethics of the American Stage and American Motion Pictures—what an ironic death for you! Acting in a Tarrington motion picture—a torture scene, when you hate them so much!"

And suddenly Tarrington was backing away from the cross.

"Nina! You three—he's waiting for you—" His wild laugh rang out. "The climax of a good picture for my eager markets—"

He was fumbling at the metal handle of his wire lash; and abruptly now I realized why he had attached it to the slithering black cord on the floor. The wire glowed red-hot from the electric current turned into it. Red-hot . . . white hot. . . .

The girls as they whirled forward, cast off their veils. The light gleamed on the naked blade of the knife each of them held . . . with flowing dark hair tossing, they stamped with barbaric dancing tread to the clashing rhythm of the music, encircling the crucified man, while ten feet away Tarrington stood like a ring-master cracking his white-hot wire lash.

Then the pallid nude girls leaped for the cross, swarming upon it, climbing one by one to embrace the crucified man. Embrace him? God! I saw them caress him, passionately, with their lips and arms and bodies—while their daggers slashed at his flesh. . . .

"More realism!" Tarrington shouted. "You damnable—" His white hot wire encircled the thigh of one of the girls—snatched her away; and Tarrington rushed at her, cuffing her. . . .

"More realism—he wants your embraces—your kisses, as he dies—"

Upon her white body the gruesome burned welt of the lash showed as he shoved her toward the cross—and she climbed again, put white arms around the dying man's neck as she pressed her lips to his—and her knife-blade ripping the flesh of his shoulder with a crimson spurt upon them both. . . .

My hands went over my face to shut out the horror at which I had no longer the strength to stare. And suddenly here in the cubby with us, came Tarrington's roaring microphonic voice:

"Bring down that new girl—and that fellow Rance—"

Bob and I were both on our feet. The Negro reached for me, and Bob went at him with a silent rush. There was the thud of Bob's fist against the brawny black chest. Then the room went into a dark chaos of horror. Against the wall I crouched as the scrambling fighting men thudded in the confined darkness. Brief chaos . . . I saw Bob hurled down by the huge Negro, his hands reaching for Bob's throat. Then Bob was up again, scrambling, backing off, lunging in a new attack. This time his fist caught the Negro full on the chin. The huge black body tumbled backward; and Bob in a frenzy was on him, raising him, hurling

him down . . . There was a gruesome crack as the black skull crashed against a wall projection. The Negro was dead. But suddenly the door clicked open. Tarrington and the other Negro were here, flinging themselves upon Bob. And then Bob went down with Tarrington and the Negro on top of him.

I fainted. I remember that I was trying to scream as I wilted into unconsciousness, with only the blurred knowledge that Tarrington picked me up, carried me. . . .

I CAME to my senses and found myself lying on the sward by the pool, with Bob's body half under me. Rope lashed his ankles and wrists. By the light of the burning brazier beside us I saw his sweating pallid face brighten as I stirred, opened my eyes, staring at him.

"You're all right, Anne? Thank God."

My thin summer clothes were limply dank on my sweat-bathed body. I tried to sit up . . . Where was Tarrington? The three girls? The tortured man on the cross? Bob and I seemed alone here in the pale hot silence of the horrible room.

"The Negro is watching us," Bob murmured. "Try and loosen my ropes . . . This damnable air—"

I could feel that the strange lightness of the air was intensified now—mingled with the perfumed scent of the brazier . . . Like breathing the fumes of a drug? . . . It whirled my senses. . . .

"My wrists," Bob muttered. "The rope —hurry—"

Frantically I fumbled under us for Bob's lashed wrists; then suddenly the Negro was bending over me.

"You are ready? Stand up—I will fix you."

A gasp of terror burst from me as he reached me, clutched and lifted me up.

"You—take your hands off her," Bob panted.

"I got to make you ready for the master—" His black fingers twitched and tore my waist—his arm pressed me against him . . . And suddenly there was a roaring voice:

"You damnable black swine—"

Tarrington came leaping from the other end of the room, from where he had shoved the cross with its crucified victim. His face was contorted, wild with frenzy as he leaped for the terrified Negro. . . .

"So you do the master's work—"

"I prepare her for you—Gawd—"

He saw the knife coming. The weird light of the brazier gleamed on its blade as the demoniac Tarrington stabbed. . . . The Negro's futile clutch missed it.

The blade sang into his glistening black chest. The black body staggered, tumbled into the pool . . . Sodden black thing lying inert; crimson welling at the chest, with the water washing it away.

And now Tarrington had seized me.

"You let—me alone," I panted. "Don't touch me—"

My knees buckled; I sank upon the sward with him beside me . . . Bob was straining helplessly at his bonds. Tarrington's hot breath was on my neck—his hands roved me—his lips nuzzled at my throat.

"You saw those girls—I need you in my pictures. New youth. New beauty—they're finished now. Not good enough any more."

"You—let me alone," I panted. Freezing terror numbed me so that all my senses whirled and the vision of his demoniac leering face swam before me . . . A panting curse came from Bob.

"You'll dance for me now?" Tarrington murmured. "You'll like it. I'll give us more air. My girls like the air here. It is stimulating—intoxicating. You heard them ask for it? The air helps them with their work. . . ."

"No," I gasped. "You let us alone—let us out of here—"

"So? You defy me?" He leaped to his feet, dragging me by one wrist until we were over Bob. Tarrington was leering as he stared down.

"You thought I didn't really remember you, Rance? Well you were wrong. That review of yours in the *Comet*—you dared assail a Tarrington production!" His snarling voice held a grisly menace. "What luck for me, having you stumble in here tonight! You make my vengeance complete—you and Blakely—"

"You—damned fiend—" Bob burst out.

"Yes—that's what Blakely said. You mean I'm a realist. Master of torture! You saw what I did to Blakely? This girl you brought here—she'll let me train her —when she hears you screaming!"

I gasped, "Yes—yes, I'll do anything you say. Anything—only don't kill him! You—you want me to show you how I can dance—train me for your pictures—"

HE straightened from Bob, and again gripped me by the wrist. "That's better. There'll be no more insubordination from you?"

"No," I murmured. "Give me music —I'll dance—"

He swung from me, striding to the wall where he pulled a switch. The faint music began throbbing. And I saw him fumbling a huge cylindrical tank—a dozen of them standing vertical in a row, partly hidden by the drapes, tanks each with a pressure valve on top. He fumbled with each of them in turn, opening the valves. In a sudden pause of the music, the tanks were hissing.

"Anne—" Bob's low voice reached me. "That's oxygen—too much of it in the air—intoxicating us—"

Tarrington was coming back now . . . Oxygen—the exhilaration of it—overstimulation of all the senses—the appetites. . . .

"You dance," Bob was swiftly murmuring. "Keep his attention—lead him across the room. I'll try—"

Then Tarrington was here. I saw the braziers burning higher now, flaring brighter with a queer tinge as the new flood of oxygen was being wafted to them. And despite my freezing, numbing terror I could feel every breath like wine surging in my lungs, my veins, tingling my body. It gave me a wild desire to laugh—and to sob and scream with terror as I kicked off my shoes, ripped down my stockings and swung into a dance of abandonment, stripping off my garments, tossing them away . . . the mirrors duplicated the slim whiteness of me . . . my black hair flowing free. . . .

Tarrington followed me, appraising me . . . I danced past the prone shapes of the three pallid girls whom suddenly I saw lying here, huddled together, staring numbly at me, breathing in the oxygen to which now they were enslaved . . . The scars of the lash, partly hidden by grease-paint, showed on their pale bodies . . . And here against the wall the cross was standing, with the blood-soaked body of Blakely hanging upon it.

Then back at the pool I saw Bob's bound figure suddenly rise up. Balanced with his lashed ankles he hopped, backing against the brazier, his bound wrists thrust into its queerly burning flame . . . I saw him twitch, writhe with the agony of his burning flesh.

"Bob—" The cry involuntarily burst from me and I stopped my dance. It warned Tarrington. He had been absorbed watching me. He turned, saw Bob, and with a roar of demoniac fury rushed forward . . . My breath stopped. I saw Bob violently twitching—then he was free—the burning ropes dropped from his wrists. His sleeves were burning; he stooped, splashed his arms in the pool, and fumbled frantically at his ankles . . . I stood swaying, staring at the turgid horror of the scene—the fren-

zied, bull-like Tarrington lunging, while still Bob stooped, frantically freeing his ankles. . . .

Then at last he straightened; met Tarrington's onslaught with a sweep of the burning brazier. Its heavy iron bowl scattered flame as Bob crashed it on Tarrington's head . . . Weird, amazing flame. In the midst of its blue tongues, I saw Tarrington fall.

FLAME gone wild. Licking blue tongues. They spread along the inflammable green-painted wood shavings of the artificial grass sward; they leaped for the filmy drapes, the artificial palms and flowers. . . Astonishing flame, fed into instant fury by this air overcharged with oxygen. The wall drapes went up in a puff; the flowers shriveled as though a blow-torch were on them . . . and then the room was a mass of flame, with Tarrington lying, still gruesomely twitching; and Bob running for me. . . .

"Anne—quick—"

The burning drapes had exposed a window. Bob pulled futilely at its big lock; then his fist crashed through the pane . . . His shoulder knocked away the ragged glass—his fists pounded and broke the locked wooden shutter . . . We saw the ground close outside. I went through the opening, with Bob after me. The roaring room behind us for just an instant seemed to hold the dying screams of those pallid girls. . . .

The dank drizzle of the night was cold on my nude body. Bob flung his jacket around me. Flame was bursting through the roof of the big frame building as we ran to where we had parked our car.

Wrapped in the auto robe, I huddled beside Bob as he dashed us down the hill and away. The fog-shrouded night behind us was a blurred yellow-red glare of flame. Gigantic funeral pyre for the fiend of the house of torture.

THE CANYON OF MISSING

A novelette of such gruesome, inexplicable terror as to make any reader lie awake in fear and trembling—for the safety of his loved ones!

CHAPTER ONE

Descent to Doom

THE whole thing seemed droll, rather a lark, until Tina and I stopped the car at the top of "The Shadow," and looked down twelve thousand feet into the Canyon of Hell Roaring Creek—so far down as to make even Chrome Mountain seem like a toy. I took a deep breath, and turned to the girl I loved.

"Maybe I shouldn't have brought you."

"Wherever you go, Locke Brette," she said, "I go, too. What's wrong?"

"The whole set-up, and it didn't come to me until just now. What are Dominicans doing away out here in the wilds of Montana? And who ever heard of able-bodied Dominicans working as common laborers anyhow?" I demanded of her.

"You insult my race," she answered, laughing. Tina was, by birth, a *Dominican*, but white, of course; descended in a direct line from the *Conquistadores*. "Besides, have you not told me that they are political refugees, and therefore, in this land, so alien to them, they must work to live?"

30

BRIDES

by ARTHUR J. BURKS
(Author of "They Call Me Killer," etc.)

Each girl who denied that evil legend must answer a weird, compelling call of the night—or lose the man she loved. Locke Brette found that they did not go to their deaths, as had been thought, but to a fate far worse—a fate that left them mindless, hollow shells; bleeding, babbling idiots!

"Yes, but why? And how did they ever hear of Chrome Mountain? How did the Boss of Chrome Mountain ever hear of them and their plight? I don't like it. I just now realize it."

"At the worst," she said, settling back, "we cannot go back. The Park of Yellowstone is closed now. In any case we must go on. . ." Her voice trailed into silence.

Again I looked down into the vast maw of the canyon. Vague, gigantic whispers came out of it. The wind, of course, but there was something eerily menacing in it. I harked back to the letter I had had from Arturo Logrono. . . ,

"There is a mystery here, an evil, bloody one, of which the world knows nothing. In Santo Domingo, long ago, you were good at mysteries. Come to investigate this one."

Good old Logrono! He had been an agent of mine when, years before, I had worked for the Department of State, in the West Indies. His letter further added that many of my Dominican friends were with the exiles under the shadow of Chrome Mountain. I had almost forgotten them. Now, all at once, I wished I really had.

But the car, as though it had a mind of its own, was already rolling down the most awe-inspiring grade in North America—that grade which was part of "The Shadow," strange name indeed for the new road that led from Red Lodge, over the Beartooth into Yellowstone Park. The Shadow! The shadow of a man—the man who had caused the road to be built. A name given in jest by a newspaper man. . . .

The downward plunge continued. I applied the brakes gently, for I knew the curves of "The Shadow." Speed on them was suicidal. A plunge over, in many places, meant a somersaulting drop of thousands of feet.

And I had no brakes!

Good God, they'd been all right, up to now. I jammed the pedal to the floor—and the car kept on gathering speed, while the hair at the base of my skull grew wet with sweat that turned icy cold. I jammed the brakes again. Nothing happened. I dared not glance aside at Tina Espaillat. She didn't know anything was wrong. But we were doomed, and I knew it, unless I could pull off a miracle.

IT WAS miles to the bottom. Some of the curves were ghastly—if taken at any great rate of speed. I saw myself in the rear vision mirror, and my face was grey. I looked ahead, where my headlights bored down "The Shadow," and my terror grew. Why, at this particular place, should my brakes have gone bad? Nobody could have touched them for we hadn't been out of the car since leaving Mammoth Hot Springs—and I'd used the brakes often since then.

Tina looked at me questioningly. I might as well tell her.

"No brakes, darling," I said, as calmly as I could. "We're heading for hell in a hand-basket!" I didn't mean to be facetious. But those words came to me, and I used them, that was all. "If I were Barney Oldfield I couldn't get safely to the bottom without brakes."

"Then," she answered, unperturbed, now having to shout to make herself heard above the screaming of the tires on the surfaced way, "you will either be better than Barney Oldfield, or we die together. Either will be all right with Tina, if there is no third alternative."

There wasn't. To the right, high walls. To the left, high walls. To the left they led to heaven, to the right to hell—or worse. The wind roared past the catapulting car. I gripped the wheel with both hands, praying for the delicate sureness of touch I knew I must have. We gathered speed.

We came to the first of the tough curves, to the left. I brought the wheel over. The car slid. I gave her the gas, wishing I didn't have to, as I needed no extra speed, and could not slow down once I had it. Yet to go into the curve, without the throttle. . . .

My right wheels kicked sand and pebbles through the two-foot high wooden railing beyond which yawned a thousand foot drop. I almost touched that barricade. For a moment I wondered if I could carom off it, slow down. But I dared not risk it. If it went, we would go with it. And if it didn't go, we might turn over it anyhow.

And all the time I kept thinking: why

did the brakes have to go at just this time? There was no sense in it. The screaming of the tires echoed back from the walls to the left, a banshee wailing in the sullen night. I glanced swiftly to the right as I managed to get onto the straightaway again—and far down I could see twinkling lights. They were still two, four—I didn't know how many —thousands of feet down, yet I could see them over the edge of the grade, and I was on the inside! Tina was literally riding the abyss! But she laughed:

"Bravo, my darling! You can do it. Let us hope there will be no blowouts!"

She didn't seem the least bit frightened, God bless her. But I swallowed my heart when she mentioned blowouts. My left rear was none too good. If it went, nothing could keep us on that serpentine grade.

I think I prayed, while all sorts of mad fancies went through my head. Dominicans in Montana! A plea for help from Arturo Logrono, who never needed the help of any man. What, in God's name, was happening to my exiled friends down yonder?

The next turn loomed ahead, this time to the right, a hairpin turn during which we must hug the inner wall—or go over the outer.

I went far out, cut back, gave her the juice—and my lights went out! No lights, and the worst curve of all, dead ahead. Ahead of us nothing but darkness—and death. Had I swung back far enough before the lights went? There was just one way, and only one, to find out—keep on going. No matter what happened, it was all I could do anyhow.

In a few seconds, during which I aged a lifetime, my eyes became partially accustomed to the lack of lights—and I could see the grade because it was white against the black of the mountains, and the night. There must have been a little moon.

BRAKES gone, lights gone—neither had ever happened to me before. And neither was an accident. I was sure of that, while just as sure that nobody could possibly have tinkered with my car. No, someone, something, intended for Tina and me to die on "The Shadow." But for God's sake, why? I'd left no enemies in Santo Domingo, and who could know that I was coming to investigate a mystery? And what was the mystery, anyhow?

Tina began to sing! Wild, lilting, carefree—with the same light-heartedness I adored in her, which had seen no wrong in her making this trip with me, prior to our marriage. She trusted me, so it was all right. And this singing was purposeful—intended to make me understand she still trusted, believed in me. I dared not look at her face, though I could detect no terror in her voice. . .

"Great Scott!" I almost flung the car off the grade, but not because of lack of brakes or lights. Something had crossed the grade, a hundred feet down—something that went on four legs, in a queer, sidelong kind of lope. It turned its eyes on us—huge greenish eyes, like those of a cat, but larger than of any cat I'd ever heard of. "What was that?"

Tina's singing broke off short, in a kind of choking sound. She spoke three words in her native tongue:

"Felipe la Chucha!"

Nonsense, I thought. "Felipe La Chucha" was the Dominican bogey-man, with whom Dominican mothers frightened their kids to sleep. He was a myth. Yet why this terror in Tina, and the explosive crying of a name for a non-existent horror?

"Rot!" I shouted. "You know there's no such animal."

"Yes, every Dominican knows it, but none would say outright that Felipe does not exist!"

My heart almost congealed. The thing

was gone. I didn't look aside as we passed the spot where both of us had seen the eyes. I didn't dare—but as we flew on down that hell grade, I could feel the green eyes upon me. Felipe la Chucha! Pictured in verbal folklore as a black man forced to walk on his hands and knees, head wagging back and forth, lips drooling saliva. A man, ageless as time, forced to travel forever thus because of his sins. So lean of flanks that the hands of a child could grasp him about the waist. But there *was* no such creature—it was simply impossible!

And yet, I rode a nightmare into Hell Roaring Canyon, and believed, as we dropped, swifter and ever swifter, that there might be something in that fantastic legend after all. . . .

God knows how we made it. I'll never know. The last was a blur during which, several times, I thought we'd left the grade and were falling. Tina, near the end, at my behest, had kept the horn going. Other drivers might be coming up. Praise God none came.

At the foot of the abysmal grade, where the road led off to the tar-roofed cabins of the chrome miners, I used the gears, almost stripping them, to bring the car, finally, to a stop.

No sooner had it happened than my left rear tire went out with a bang. I just sat there, scarcely breathing. Tina didn't say anything, and I knew why. She'd never expected to come this far. She didn't believe it, any more than I did. We were afraid to speak for fear we'd realize we'd passed from life to death so quickly we hadn't been aware of the transition.

"Locke Brette! Locke Brette!"

I let my breath out explosively. Anyhow, I was alive, and that shout came from the lips of Arturo Logrono. Now I looked at Tina. She had fainted dead away, now that the danger—at least on "The Shadow"—was past.

BROWN-FACED Logrono came out of the night, and put his head into the door of the car. He was panting. His eyes were big. He glanced across me at Tina. Then he held up both hands.

"No, Locke, no! Do not tell me! It is impossible that you have bring Tina!"

"She is here. I thought only of an outing, a vacation—"

"Outing! Vacation! An outing in hell, my friend—a vacation in Bardo! I do not tell all, lest you do not come—and since I do not, you think it safe to bring Tina."

I held my breath, while waves of terror poured over me. I had to find out things. There was one way to do it.

"Arturo," I said, "my brakes went bad. My lights went out, and we saw something on the grade, and Tina cried out that it was Felipe La Chucha. God knows how I ever managed the grade."

"Felipe la Chucha!" repeated Arturo. "God, Locke, it can't be! The Kookura is here already, and now comes Felipe la Chucha. . ."

I even forgot the horror of the grade at his mention of the Kookura, another folklore monster—which made two of them. One laughed at them by day, but by night, at the foot of "The Shadow," under Chrome Mountain, with the Canyon's roaring breath bathing ones body, heart, and soul, it was a different matter. But I tried to laugh.

"The Kookura, who walks on mountain-tops, and gathers up bad children and devours them. . . . Such utter nonsense!"

"Yes, my friend? Then explain this: if it is not the Kookura, which we are coming to believe—which maybe, all the time, all Dominicans believe in—*what is it that, during the past two weeks, has carried away four of our young women and devoured them?*"

"Young women?" I said, foolishly. Then I looked at Tina. She had snapped out of it in time to hear. Her face was grey with terror. She too, in her childhood, had been frightened half out of her wits by tales of the Kookura, and Felipe La Chucha. *Young women!*

Tina was twenty.

"I am leaving, going on into Red Lodge," I told Logrono.

"Impossible," he said, with ghastly simplicity. "Did you meet anyone on the grade? No! Because nothing moves, and lives, in the canyon after nightfall, my friend—save in terror of hell that comes down from the mountains, and roams to and fro in them. One thing I beg of you: if danger of any sort threatens Tina— *slay her with whatever you have at hand. . ."*

I smelled the gasoline, then, wondered why I hadn't before, I got out of the car, went behind it. My last gasoline was just spilling out of what might have been a bullet hole in the bottom of the tank. And I wouldn't have *walked* to Red Lodge, through that canyon, for all the wealth in Chrome Mountain. No, not even though reason told me that nothing like the Kookura, and Felipe La Chucha, existed save in fancy.

For many people believed in both, and what men and women believe in so completely—especially when they are frightened—*may come into being because of that belief!*

We guarded Tina between us as we walked to the black blotches under Chrome Mountain that were the shacks of the miners.

CHAPTER TWO

Shadows Under Chrome

IT WAS rather pitiful, and heartbreaking the way those Dominicans gathered about Tina and me, in the house of Logrono, who acted as *jefe* of the miners. Logrono told me briefly how they had come to be in that place.

"We are driven out of Santo Domingo because we are not in sympathy with certain powerful *politicos* and cannot compromise with our consciences. We leave with only the money we have in our hands. In New York I read advertisements which speak of work out here. I see it is a good place to hide, where enemies will not find us. I see the man whom they call the Boss of Chrome Mountain, tell him of our plight. We are, he say, just the people he wishes to work for him. We are here. Chrome Mountain is very rich. We strike most of it two weeks ago. That same night the . . . the. . ."

"Kookura?" I asked softly.

Many heads nodded. They were all terrified to death. Tina swayed. I touched her arm to steady her. She smiled.

"Nonsense," she said, "there is no such thing as—"

"Don't! Don't!" came in a ghastly scream from one of the brown-skinned women. "To deny that there is a Kookura . . . well, all who died have denied him, and they are dead! Maybe, even before I stop you, you say too much."

Tina's smile faded. Her lips were white. Fear crawled in my heart, too. . . . I studied all those faces, saw a man named Carlos Palos. I spoke to him.

"You knew we were coming, Carlos?"

"Yes, Locke Brette."

"I killed your brother when I was an agent in Santo Domingo. Does his blood cry for vengeance?"

"He played a game. He lost," said Carlos Palos, grimly. "I have no desire for revenge."

I believed him. "And you, Pedro Gallo, whom I sent to prison? You Juan Silvas, whose brother faced a firing squad because of evidence I found. Do you desire my death?"

"We did," they said in effect. "But that was long ago."

I believed them, too. Besides, the horror had started before Arturo had even written me. No, the attempt on Tina and me, at the top of the grade—but *had* it been an attempt? Yes! Bad brakes, no lights, a blowout that just failed, a punctured gas tank. They couldn't all have been coincidence. I was cold to the depths of my soul, cold with dread of what was to come.

"This Kookura may be a man-eating mountain lion. . ."

I stopped without going further, stopped because of the expressions on their faces. The men exchanged glances, and it was a woman who said grimly:

"Since when does a mountain lion mate with a woman before he slays her."

Tina stifled a moan. The vast canyon seemed to creep in closer to us. The lights flickered on the table about which we were standing and seated. There was a new, deep-throated sound to the canyon's "breathing. . . ."

"But if the women stay inside after nightfall . . ." I began again.

They exchanged glances again—and with shocking, horrible suddenness, it came. A long, savage, bloodcurdling shriek from somewhere under the towering shadow of Chrome Mountain, against which this cluster of huts was built. The cry of a woman in agony. Instantly the men looked over their women, looked at me.

"Our women are all here, with us," said Logrono. "That sound—"

"Was as I expected," I said, "the hunting cry of a cougar—"

I got no further, for right then one of the women, a young girl, jumped to her feet. Her eyes bulged horribly. There was a drool of saliva on her gibbering lips. Her head rolled from side to side as though she listened for the cry to be repeated. Then, in her native Spanish, she said:

"The cry was for me! I must go. I denied the Kookura. Now it demands payment. If I do not go, it takes one I love."

She whirled, and before a hand could touch her, opened the door and dashed out into the night. The Dominicans stopped at the door as though pushed back by invisible hands. I grabbed a rifle from nails on the wall, made sure it was fully loaded. I snapped at Logrono, "If anything happens to Tina while I'm gone, I'll kill you!"

THEN I dashed out after the girl, whose name was Manuella Costa, young wife of Horacio Costa. I saw her hurrying up the incline which led to the cliff of Chrome Mountain. She went swiftly. I called after her to come back, but she was deaf to my call. The night closed in until I pursued Manuella through a black tunnel, her white dress the beacon that guided me. And fast as I went, she drew swiftly away from me. I kept on calling, in vain. I even thought of attempting to stop her with a bullet through the leg, but I didn't dare. Now, I know it would have made no difference. . . . She followed a rough trail that I guessed led to the mouth of one of the mines. There were tall trees to right and left through which the wind raged. I glanced aside now and again, saw greenish eyes, as though the mountain were alive with cats, but I told myself it was my over-wrought imagination.

Then came the scream. I ran faster, turned a bend in the trail. I could still see the white dress of Manuella, or part of it. We had left the huts a quarter of a mile behind us—as far away as the moon. Something towered over Manuella. She had stopped, as though attempting to go further were useless.

"Take me," I heard her say, when she stopped screaming, "but spare Horacio!"

I stumbled, fell, lay for a moment stunned. I had struck my head against a rock. I fought to get to my feet. I looked ahead. Manuella was down. I saw the towering figure over her—whose shape I cannot even now define—in dreadful movement. Savage, exultant sounds came from it. I raised the rifle and fired twice, as fast as I could. Maybe I forgot about holding high when shooting uphill, for I heard my bullets go zinging off into the night. I hurried on, clutching the rifle.

And when I was close, the thing disappeared. Just like that. One moment it was there, then it was gone. I stood over Manuella, looked down at her. Her white dress was no longer white. It had been ripped off her. It was stained with blood. Her breasts had been ripped to shreds. Her abdomen was a surgeon's horror. I knelt beside her.

"Manuella, what was it?"

"The Kookura," she whispered, "but Horacio is safe!"

"Did he—" But I stopped with the question half asked, because she was dead. There was no question of "devouring" her. I'd prevented it, perhaps, if devouring had been planned by—whatever it was. But bestial lust had had its way, and fangs, or talons, or claws, had done the rest.

I held the rifle with my left hand, hoisting Manuella to my back in the fireman's lift. Cold fury burned in me. I started back down the trail. Then I stopped stockstill.

"Locke! Locke! Are you all right?"

Tina's voice, filled with terror! And it was coming up the trail toward me. I froze in my tracks, unable for a few brief, ghastly seconds, to find words to shout back at her. Then I managed it.

"Tina, go back! Go back! Run for your life! Get back inside!"

There was no answer. Maybe she was too frightened to answer. Then, I heard footfalls in the pebbles on the trail, returning to the cabins. I listened, forgetting the grisly terror all about me, praying to hear her reach a cabin, enter, slam the door. Those sounds never came.

The running footfalls ceased abruptly. There was no sound, no scream, nothing. It was as though Tina, halfway back to

comparative safety, had been snatched into nothingness—*by what?* But that was silly, absurd. I had misjudged distance, time, sound. She'd got back to the cabins. I started running again. Manuella's body bounced on my back, and her warm blood seeped through my clothing, wet my trembling, crawling skin.

I REACHED the big cabin, burst in, forgetting Horacio Costa. When he saw Manuella he went berserk. He jerked the rifle from my hands, dashed out the door. I looked around the room. Tina wasn't there.

"She ran after you," said Logrono, "before anybody could stop her!"

"And you brave bullies didn't follow her!" But what was the use of accusing anyone in this community, so utterly ruled by terror?

I lowered the crimson body of Manuella to the floor. Women gathered about it, exclaiming in horror. One woman began the Dominican lament for the dead, the most doleful sound in all creation. The others picked it up and presently I could stand it no longer.

Unarmed this time, I was out on the trail again, hunting for Costa and Tina. But it was Tina's name I called, over and over again until I was hoarse. I stumbled over the rifle Horacio had snatched from me. The stock was smashed and bloody, the barrel bent in an arc. Further on I found Horacio Costa, his skull hammered to a jelly.

"Tina! Tina! For God's sake answer me!"

Answer me she did, then, from somewhere in the woods to the south, and her answer flooded my soul with horror.

"Go 'way, Locke! Go 'way! I don't want you. . . ." That was what she said.

Her words broke off in strange, horrible moans. First I thought they were moans of pain. But my flesh crawled with the sudden knowledge that painful, bestial ecstasy was in them somehow. I could hear sounds of a struggle, the thump of bodies falling to the ground. Then the strange moaning cries of a *man!*

Visions of what must be happening to Tina, there in the darkness, drove me as mad as sight of Manuella had driven Horacio Costa.

I flung myself against the wall of the night, and the sighing woods, as though I had been a company of soldiers attacking a fortress. The trees hurled me back. The moans I had heard fell into silence—trembling, ghastly silence.

Then I burst into a patch of moonlight and saw here—saw her just as a huge, nebulous form rose to its feet, bearing her nude, unconscious body over grotesque shoulders, and dashed on deeper into the woods.

"Stop you beast! I'll tear your heart out! If you harm her. . ."

But words were useless. I could hear the panting gasps of whatever the thing was—and there was triumph in the sound.

It seemed to be headed directly for the cliff itself. I managed a fresh burst of speed when I saw the black opening of what might be the mine of Chrome—and something struck me on the base of the skull.

Stars exploded through absymal darkness in which there was nothing at all. I awoke in the midst of the "dead" who had vanished from the cabins of the expatriate miners.

CHAPTER THREE

Where Are the Dead?

I LIFTED my throbbing head. My hands and feet were bound behind me and I could scarcely breathe. My body with bathed in the sweat of horror. Deep in the bowels of the earth we were—and this was no new working, but obviously an old, abandoned mine. Dug by men of yesterday who had been seeking gold, no doubt—to whom chrome had meant nothing whatever.

I knew at once that of the "vanishers," only Manuella Costa had died. If I hadn't gone after her, she would have been alive —but I was glad she was not. For what words could picture what I saw, there in the old mine?

The early diggers had run into something strange, deep in the heart of Chrome Mountain. They had dug into the stratified graves of elder time, and what they had found they had left standing, as a support to the roof of a vast room they had hollowed out. Maybe what they saw in that jagged, misshapen column had frightened them away.

Ancient mankind! A whole family of human beings who must have lived on the earth before Chrome Mountain had vanished under the sea, and then had risen again when the earth rebuilt its mountains. They looked like monster apes— but their faces were undeniably human, indelibly petrified there in the ageless rocks. Two men, two women, a ghastly child. They looked like idols out of hell. Leering mouths, holes for eyes. The miners had made sure of the nature of their find before they had fled in terror from ghosts millions of years old.

And now, modern beasts had turned the vast room into an unbelievable shrine! Candles flickered in countless rocky niches, and their flames cast the shadows of the ancient family on the rocky walls, unbelievably hideous. And all around that grisly column ranged the four lost women!

Those four naked, voluptuous women, were stark, staring mad.

I looked at the men who held them prisoners. I could scarcely make them out, save that they were white. I guessed that something had been done to their faces, for their eyes bugged, their lips drooled, and their teeth were like fangs.

I got a hunch from those clothes. These hard, huge white men were the Chrome miners whom the innocent Dominicans had displaced in the diggings—and they were out for a grisly revenge; revenge on the interlopers, mixed with lustful orgies beyond the power of pen to describe.

And now two men picked me up, carried me around the room until I could see—Tina Espaillat, pinioned against those grisly petrified figures like a white statue crucified!

There was blood on her lips. Her head rolled on her shoulders and low moans escaped her. Towering over her was one of the stone men, and it looked to me as though smoke came out of his nostrils.

That figure, and all the others, even that of the child, seemed to be inciting the followers of whatever ungodly cult this might be to orgies beyond conception.

Another man came, with several whips in his dirty, huge hand. He gave a whip to each of four men. Then he spoke:

"Do you, Tina Espaillat, take to husband this dawn man?"

There was laughter in the question, a hideous travesty on the ceremony of marriage. Tina did not answer.

"Do not be afraid to answer, lovely Tina. For it is marriage by proxy, only —and one of us will serve in the dawn man's stead!"

I WRITHED and twisted in my bonds, until they cut into my flesh like fire. I swore. The speaker then raised his whip and struck. A red weal appeared on the face of Tina, and ran down between her breasts. The fellow had struck downward as though the whip had been a knife. The weal began to bleed.

A gibbering cry rose from the other men. The sight of blood drove them to frenzy. The four women, as though the gibbering made them remember, as nothing else would make them remember, ever, began to cry softly. I had never heard anything so heart-chilling as their hopeless, fearful weeping. The man with the whip struck again.

Tina cringed, but did not cry out. I tried to roll toward the man with the whip. Another man came, put his foot on my head, held me down, helpless, writhing—but so that I still could see.

Tina screamed as the beast struck again. The crying of the women rose higher, and higher too, the gibbering of the men.

Now the man with the whip snapped at the others: "Lay on! What is more desirable than a woman writhing in unbearable torture?"

The other whips were going now, and every blow crashed hard upon my own soul.

"Now," said the spokesman, "cut them down! And what say you? Shall the candles be left lighted?"

"Yes! Yes!"

I would see the finale of this thing then, and never be able to shut it out of my mind. Now Tina was mumbling. . . .

"Kookura! Kookura! Felipe La Chucha! Felipe La Chucha! That they should so blaspheme the harmless creatures of our childhood! Come to us, to avenge us, and yourselves! Come! Come!"

Tina, in a strange, mad way, was praying—praying to the Kookura and to Felipe La Chucha, begging them to help their own. My brain whirled. How had these men, who probably had never heard of Santo Domingo, thought of the Kookura and Felipe La Chucha, to fill the Canyon of Hell Roaring Creek with terror? And how, now, did Tina pray to them both? It made my flesh crawl anew.

Tina spoke in Spanish, and the whip cut across her lips until she made an end of her delirious prayer. Knives flashed, and nude women toppled to the floor of the cavern of horror. They were still crying, and now all of them were writhing with the pain of the whips—and four of them from countless old wounds that had been reopened. The crying and the writhing drove the men still madder.

Motive was not lacking. Hard rock men are hard. Some of them go for weeks and months without sight of women.

And the Boss of Chrome Mountain had brought in outsiders, who in turn brought women as voluptuous and fiery as any to be found in the world. Thus the ousted miners could kill two birds with one stone—avenge themselves on the interlopers, and appease their own hell-born lusts.

Tina fell close to me. The man whose foot held my head down, moved away.

Maybe there was some slight sense of shame in some of them, near the end, for at the last someone yelled hoarsely that the candles be doused.

A man stood over Tina, gazing down on her beauty which even the marks of the whip could not hide. His lips worked. They were loose and flabby. The light in his eyes might well have been born in this hell pit.

ONE by one the candles went, and slowly Stygian darkness possessed the pit. Darkness which had gripped the bowels of the earth here for years beyond the conception of human minds. As the light faded I saw the shapes of the broken women fade. I watched the men, as, impatient, like beasts held carelessly in leash, they began to bend toward the women. . . .

And when the last candle went out, yells of hideous desire thundered in the pit. And those yells would drown out any other yells that might sound. I rolled over, until my face came in contact with human flesh. I used, then, the only weapons I had. My teeth.

A hand struck at me as I rolled against legs that were knotted bands of muscle—now nude in the dark. When the hand touched my face I fastened my teeth in the fatty palm, next to the little finger, and bit until my teeth met through the flesh. I would never let go, I told myself.

My enemy screamed. His free hand belabored me with blows that might have been dealt by bludgeons. But I clung, while stars burst and flamed in my head. The man shouted words.

"Let go, you ———, or I'll batter you to pieces! What do you care about the woman, when you won't live to leave here?"

I felt something rub against me. A hand—a *small* hand—touched the back of my head. Just so, often, had Tina touched me with both hands when she had lifted her lips to mine.

Then the hand was withdrawn. The monster still struck out at me. He flung himself about. Then, all at once, I heard the unmistakable sound a knife makes when it drives through skin and flesh and muscle. The man screamed again. Again and again I heard the knife go home.

Then the man rolled onto me, limp, and for the second time that night I felt hot blood cascade over my tortured flesh.

Then, the knife was busy again—and I was free.

Tina came into my arms for a moment. The dead man quivered against my legs. I clung to Tina, she to me—and so primordal was the suggestion of this ancient charnel house, that then and there I desired Tina, and her desire answered mine.

But we both knew, and feared this horror. We could not linger. . . .

I took the knife from her hand, whispered to her,

"Get close against the rock where you were fastened. Let the dawn man guard you until I come back to you!"

She drew away from me, her whole body shaking with pain. I straightened, hesitating not at all in what I had to do. I listened for the nearest bestial sounds. I gripped the knife tightly in my right hand, and moved toward that sound. In this place it would be easy—for already I knew where each man was, because I knew where each unhappy woman had fallen.

I moved to the right, my left hand extended in case one of the enemy stood upright.

My feet touched a writhing mound of bestiality.

I stooped, raised the knife and plunged it downward. . . .

CHAPTER FOUR

What of Tomorrow?

I MYSELF must have been a thing of horror for the next few minutes. But I did not care. Even today I have no regret, save that each of those evil men had but one life to pay for the horror he had caused.

This is how, panting, filled with the desire to rend and maim, I did it. I felt for a hairy head, fastened my hand in it. Maybe the man thought the woman with him clutched at him in mad response to his lust. When he discovered differently—it was too late.

As his head turned in my hand, my right fist, holding the knife of dreadful execution, knew the exact distance to his throat. And his blood did not further sully the body of the woman.

Three were left, so when I was sure, I moved on to the next. Maybe the sounds of horror had lessened a little, I don't know. But when I came to the third man I knew—and did to him as I had done the first. I struck with savage glee, mouthing my fury in animal snarls.

Two were left.

Two minutes sufficed for them. Then the only sound left was the moaning of the women, invisible there in the grisly, impenetrable dark. I felt I had to hurry. There might be others somewhere, approaching the mine even now. Down in the cabins, I knew, Logrono and the others were cowering, sure in their frightened minds that Tina and I were dead—that everybody who had left the cabins, gone into the night, had gone for good.

I was finished. I went back to Tina now. I took my handkerchief and with all the tenderness of which I was capable, blindfolded her. She must not see what I intended to see—and gloat over. Maybe it was the sight of my gloating I wished to deny her, I don't know. For at the moment I was as much a beast as the men I had destroyed.

"Stand here, beloved," I told her. "We are safe, now."

Then I went through the pockets of the discarded clothing of the dead until I found matches. I fumbled along the walls until I found a candle and lighted it. It was long enough for my purpose.

Now I turned back and looked down at each of my victims. I couldn't help the horrible laughter that burst from my lips at what I saw. My work had been good.

Five dead men. I had struck with maniacal fury, for I had all but severed the heads of two of them from their bodies. I looked at the whips they had dropped, and the insane desire came to me to give them to the moaning women, and bid them cut and slash at the bodies of the slain.

But I controlled this hideous desire. The whips could not hurt the dead. Now, what to do with the living? And what, for them, of tomorrow? What would their men feel for them, when I took them back, and they knew? If they ever did, for all four were mad.

I did a thing that seemed cruel to those four brutally used, mad women. I pulled them to their feet, commanded them to stand. I slapped their faces until they whimpered—but they stood. Then, as tenderly as possible, I fastened their wrists together, making hideous prisoners of the four, with strips cut with the weapon of execution from the clothing of the dead.

Tina and I were ready to take the four pitiful ones back to their husbands. Would those husbands have them back? Would *any* man, however guiltless the woman, desire her after. . . .

What had happened to Tina?

THAT first attack in the woods, when she had been snatched off the trail! Those ghastly minutes I had been separated from her. Which man had captured her, and what. . . .

I closed my mouth against questions. I shut my soul against hideous shadows. I steeled my heart against memory.

"Come, Tina," I said, "let us lead these poor ones back."

"Yes, Felipe!" she whispered.

I grabbed her shoulders, shook her. Was she delirious again?

"I am not Felipe La Chucha," I told her. "There is no such thing. No Kookura. . ."

"But I prayed," she said simply, "and my prayer was answered. Maybe you are not Felipe now; but for several moments, while you meted out punishment, you were both Felipe and the Kookura. But we shall forget—if *you* can forget!— and never mention either's name!"

Her calm statement gave me a fresh chill. *Was* there something to Dominican folklore? Had I become, for the moments of the slaughter of the beasts in that hell pit, the incarnation of Felipe La Chucha and the Kookura? Had the prayers of Tina Espaillat brought their spirits winging into my soul, to send me berserk?

The answer, I believe, is yes! . . .

Tina and I started leading the four down the mountainside. Tina wore nothing, and now the blindfold was off. I doubt if she realized she was nude. What did it matter, anyhow? Now and again she moaned—with the pain, I thought,

though I could scarcely fight down the clamoring question: "Does she moan with pain, *or with memory of something worse?"*

Slowly we followed that trail down. Now and again the terror of my last trip this way bore down upon me, and I thought the horror still not ended. For several times I saw the eyes, the balls of lambent, greenish flames that seemed ever to glow in the wooded dark. The last time I saw them they were moving up the mountain, toward that mine mouth.

And so, we came to the cabins . . . and went in. And not a man there seemed concerned by the nudity of the women. And I need not have doubted the men, either. Maybe it was fortunate that Horacio Costa was dead, for he would not mourn his Manuella.

The four husbands of the four broken women stared. Then, tears starting from their eyes, each stepped forward, lifted his own as though she were a babe—as soon as I had cut the bonds—and stepped with her to a chair. Their tears kept streaming down their faces as they wrapped their tortured wives in what clothing other women handed them.

I turned to Tina, to whom someone had given a sleazy, dirty dress—but in which she was utterly lovely despite the marks of the whip—and maybe there were tears on my cheeks, too. But when I held out my arms she shook her head.

"Your job is not yet finished, Locke," she said. "And while you finish it there will be time to think. If then, you hold out your arms. . ."

She was right.

"Come, Arturo," I said, "we're going to find the full explanation for this Kookura and Felipe La Chucha business. Neither roams the woods now, and it is safe to go out."

I DIDN'T express contempt in my words, and Logrono knew it. In his way, perhaps, he had a kind of courage. Had he been sure that men were back of the horror in the Canyon, he would have faced a dozen of them with his hands, feet and teeth. But the Kookura and Felipe La Chucha—those, he had not been able to face.

"The women," I told him grimly, when we were on the trail back to the grisly pit, "believed in the Kookura and Felipe. They hypnotized themselves into believing that the cries that came out of the night were commands they dared not disobey. Childhood beliefs are strange things, Arturo."

"Yes," he said, "yes."

"And the cries always were," I told him, "the cries of hunting cougar. I know. They sound like women in torment."

"But your brakes, the tire, the gas tank. . ."

"Tell me, Arturo," I continued, "is there a way to reach the summit of the grade without traveling by the road?"

"Why yes, of course, a trail cowboys used to use. . ."

"And before I came you often discussed my coming? That when I came I would solve the mystery?"

"Why yes, often. We all looked forward to your coming."

"Then it is simple. Night after night men listened outside your cabins, while through your windows they feasted their eyes on your women, and made their selections. Then, when Tina and I were due, one of them went up that trail and waited. There was one spot where a driver would be almost sure to stop—the summit of the grade, where the first view of the canyon bursts on one, where one naturally brakes down, and stops for a little time to drink in the grandeur. For those few moments he can think of nothing else, is conscious of nothing else.

"That happened to me tonight. A man lay in wait. It doesn't matter which man. My car stopped. He slid in under it, did something to my brakes, the wires of my lights. On his back in the road, under the car, he waited until I started. Then he drove the blade of a knife into my gas tank, and slashed at the nearest tire. Then he laughed as I gathered speed. . ."

"But you said you saw Felipe La Chucha on the grade. . ."

"*Tina* said that, Arturo. My thought was of a cougar, a mountain lion. I'm sure of it now, for he prowls around here. I've seen his eyes several times tonight. . ."

Logrono and I carried flashlights. He exclaimed when I led him to the cave mouth. I took the lead in. I smelled again the odor of blood. Again I felt the urge to strike, to smash, and maim. I was glad that Logrono could not see the beast in my face.

We turned twice, following that tunnel —until we came to the big room.

"Now, Arturo," I said, "look!"

I swept the light about the place. First it touched the ancient family in stone. Then I lowered it . . . . stopped, almost screamed.

For I had found the eyes again. Those greenish eyes glared into the beam of my flash. A great cat sprawled on the body of one of the men I had slain. A spitting snarl burst through its dripping, bloody fangs.

The cougar did not leap, but gave us warning that death would be our portion if we interfered with its feasting. . . .

"Come away, Arturo," I said, softly. "I couldn't have thought of a better way to dispose of those beasts—than by the fangs of a beast only a little less ferocious than themselves!"

And so I went back to Tina, and without the slightest hesitation held out my arms again.

THE END

The
CORPSE
FACTORY

by

Arthur Leo Zagat
Author of "Death Dancers," etc.

*Living derelicts, cast ruthlessly aside
by the power that had maimed
them, they formed in time an Army
of the Damned—a near-dead, moaning legion, whose fleshless faces and
sightless eyes were as fuel to the
flames that swept an innocent girl
and man through seven fearsome
hours of hell on earth!*

Complete Horror Novel

THE road was wide and well-sur-
faced, as it would have to be for
the trucks I had seen back there in
Roton, the huge green tank trucks that
brought their loads of Neosite fifty miles
to the nearest railroad. But on either side
the light of my headlamps sprayed out
into a blank nothingness, and when the
way curved their beam swept over flat
swampland, vacant and desolate. The
humid air, too, was heavy with a rank
miasma, an odor of putrescence. I felt
seeping away from me the elation with
which I had started toward the biggest
job of my career, the superintendency, no
less, of the plant whose cheap and super-
efficient product was driving other motor
fuels from the market. I tried to shrug
off my growing depression, but it weighed

on me more and more heavily as the car that had been waiting for me at the shipping point bored on into the night.

The highway lifted in a gradual rise whose crest was sharply defined against the pale glimmer of an overcast sky. A chemical engineer should have no imagination, but I had to fight off an eerie feeling that there, just ahead, was the end of the world; that beyond was sheer emptiness. My skin prickled as I saw a formless black excrescence on that ominous skyline, a black and brooding blob of too solid shadow. . . . Then I neared and the anomalous bulk took on human contour. Almost involuntarily my foot lifted from the gas pedal, shifted to the brake and slowed the car to a stop. I leaned out.

The fellow my headlight revealed was seated on the ground at the roadside, his long thin arms clasped around gangling, up-bent knees. I judged him to be young, about eighteen, but there was ageless vapidity in his leathery, hollow-cheeked face, dull incuriousness that was not youthful in the lackluster eyes with which he met my own. I could read not even the intelligence of an animal in his countenance; somehow it was flat and featureless as the very swamp from which he appeared to have sprung.

"How far to Newville, buddy?" I called to explain my halt.

He looked at me, unblinking. He didn't reply, but the narrow rim of his forehead wrinkled under his stringy, unkempt black hair. I repeated my question in a louder voice, as if mere noise could penetrate his stupidity.

"Five er ten mile." His husky voice was quite inflectionless and his lips scarcely moved.

"Thanks." I couldn't keep the sarcasm out of my tone. "That tells me a lot." I might as well have spared the effort; he seemed already to have forgotten my presence, was staring unseeingly through my car. I trod on the starter button . . . .

Then, from somewhere beyond, a moaning wail sounded—low, muffled, but vibrant with an agony that was somehow uncomprehending. Like the plaint of a hurt cat it welled in a crescendo of suffering.

"Good Lord!" I gritted. "What's that?"

"Mom."

The youth showed not the slightest flicker of interest.

I tried to peer into the blank wall of darkness past my headlights. "What's the matter with her?" I asked.

"Nothin'. It's 'Lije. He's dyin'."

"'Lije?"

"M' brother." There was a slight tinge of expression in his tone this time, of exasperation at my continued questioning.

I switched the car lights off. The wail came again—unutterably sorrowful. The blackness faded. I saw a bulk of darker shadow, ahead and to the left of the road, and a pale rectangle of flickering yellow luminance that might be a window. "Maybe she needs help," I said sharply. "A doctor."

"Ain't no doctor kin stop the Peelin's. Ain't no doctor nigher'n Roton anyways." He sat like a clod, motionless, uncaring.

I slid to the ground and made for what was now defined as a crazily leaning hut. Maybe I couldn't do any good, but I couldn't go on without finding out. I'm not built that way.

My feet sank into soft, sucking mire, found a narrow path of muddy but firmer ground. There was no lock on the drab door of unpainted rough boards and I pulled it open. A stench of decayed food, human filth, was febrilely warm around me. There was another scent, pungent and foul, that I could not identify. I stepped into a cluttered, grimy room where one feeble candle flickered on a debris strewn table. The beastlike wailing twisted me to a corner.

THE woman was on her knees, crouched over what was at my first glance a flat pile of dirt-colored rags. The garment she wore was pulled tight over the abject curve of her back and I could trace the humped line of her spine showing through. Her hair was scraggly, streaked black and gray; and broken, black-rimmed fingertips curved clawlike over the thin lines of her shoulders.

Apparently she had not heard my entrance. I moved toward her, my lips parting to speak. And froze as I glimpsed that over which she moaned.

It wasn't a face on that pallet of rags, not such a face as even the foulest of nightmares could present. Nor was it a skull. That at least is bone, clean and dead. This was stripped clear of flesh, except where some blackened shreds still clung, but the bared muscles were there, and white threadings of nerves, and there was a quivering of agonized life over the blurred surface. The eyelids were gone. From the dark pits they should have covered, sightless balls stared a chalky, translucent white. Seared lip edges were eaten raggedly away from a yellow, rotted grin. And the head had neither nose nor ears. The rest, mercifully, was hidden from sight by a dirt-crusted, tattered blanket.

I must have made some sound, though I was not aware of it, for the woman turned. Had it not been for the other, her countenance might have inspired horror in me, so lined with suffering, so emaciated it was. Strands of bedraggled, grimy hair fell across her brow, and from behind them her eyes glittered, ratlike. Something like a rat, too, there was in the furtive startlement of her expression, in the snarling lift of her thin lips.

"What d'yer want?" she squeaked.

"Your son told me you were in trouble," I managed to speak—steadily, I hoped. "Is there anything I can do?"

"Who're you?"

"Thorndal's new superintendent. I was—" The blaze of hate in her face cut me off. She leaped to her feet and shrieked:

"Thorndal! Git out! Thet's whut yer kin do. Git out o' here. He's done ernough ter me, he an' his devils!" She snatched up a carving knife from the table. "Git out 'fore I fergit I'm a God-fearin' woman an' use this on yer."

I dodged to the door. "But—but—"

"But nothin'. Ye'll git th' other too— Zeke'll be thar tomorrer! But he ain't yers yit. Not ternight." She lunged at me, the knife sweeping in a long arc, and I dived out, slamming the ramshackle panel behind me. I missed the path, and as I floundered through the patch of swamp between hovel and road the door flung open behind me. "I hope yer mother has to look at yer," the virago shrilled after me, "a month from terday." Cackling, obscene laughter rattled in the dark.

I lurched into my car, kicked blindly at the starter. The roadside watcher, Zeke, had not moved, had not even turned his head to the clamor. But he spoke now, above the roar of my motor, and I throttled down to listen to him.

"Thar wuz a nut loose on yer license plate," he said. "I fixed it."

Gears rasped and I hurtled away from there as if ten thousand devils from Hell pursued me.

CHAPTER TWO

Eyes of Pity

THE road along which I fled curved in a long line, dipped, and rose again. The land to the left rose with it, and here and there a tree showed, gaunt and somehow solitary against the brooding quarter-light of the horizon. I realized that the ground must be firmer here, firm enough to support the stills and gigantic retorts shown on the blueprints Andrew Thorndal had displayed to me.

He hadn't told me much about the process in the interview at which I had been engaged, at a salary startling in these days of slow recovery. There were non-patentable steps, he had explained, in the manufacture of Neosite that his competitors would pay hugely to purloin. "I'll go over the whole thing thoroughly when you get out to Newville," he had rumbled. "Where I can make sure the secrets won't be blabbered."

There had been a challenge, and a threat, in his steely eyes when he had said that across our luncheon table at the Chemist's Club in New York. I had met the challenge frankly. "My first principle is loyalty to my employers, Mr. Thorndal," I had responded. "Through self-interest if nothing else. A man in my profession who does not adhere to that policy finds his career ended very quickly."

The full lips had hardened grimly under his close-clipped gray mustache. "Stick to that, Sutton," he said, "and we'll get along. Otherwise—we're pretty well cut off from the world at Newville and I have my own methods of dealing with—traitors."

Cut off was right! I had asked him why there was no railroad spur to the plant. Even then it seemed to me his reply was evasive. Newville was surrounded by a thirty-five mile stretch of bottomless swamp land; there were no other factories or towns in the region. But the tremendous production of his own industry would have rendered a one-track branch line profitable, and the well-built highway along which I was now journeying could not have presented any lesser engineering difficulties than the

building of a railroad. I wondered now whether his isolation was not deliberate.

And my thoughts returned to the scene I had just left. The flesh-stripped face of the dying man had not vanished from my inward vision; it will, I am afraid, never entirely disappear. What disease could have produced that condition? I am somewhat of an amateur physician—one has to be in the outlands to which my work takes me—but I could think of none. It wasn't leprosy—that turns the sloughing tissue an unholy white. Cold rippled along my backbone. *Was it a disease at all?*

A cluster of lights came into view ahead. This must be Newville, the small town Thorndal had built for his truck-drivers and skilled mechanics. My headlight picked up a barrier across the road, striped black and white for visibility, a tall, green-uniformed figure standing in front of it. I skidded to a stop, and the guard came alongside my running-board. There was a revolver in the hand he lifted to the sill of the open window to my left, and his heavy-jowled visage glowered forbiddingly.

"Who are yuh, and what do yuh want?" he demanded.

I flushed at his overbearing manner, but one doesn't argue with a man whose gun snouts at one's diaphragm. "Stanley Sutton, officer," I answered. "I'm the new superintendent at the works."

"Where's yuhr pass?"

I remembered a card Thorndal had handed me at our parting and which I had inattentively stuffed into my wallet. I got it out. The man scrutinized it, handed it back. "That looks okay," he muttered. "Yuh're to park yuhr car in the garage an' wait there for orders."

"I thought I was to put up in the town. Why—?"

"I don't know nothin'." A secretive veil appeared to drop across his face.

"That's what I was told to tell yuh, an' that's all I know about it." He didn't seem to be much impressed by my new dignity. "The garage is straight on, 'bout a quarter mile. All right, Joe."

HE STEPPED back and a dim-seen figure to one side bent and seemed to be operating a lever of some kind. The barrier lifted jerkily, and I let my clutch in. Surely the guarding of a secret process did not require an armed road patrol a mile or more from the plant where it was being carried on. What was I getting into? I fought down a sudden impulse to turn the car around and make for Roton and civilization.

Would God I had obeyed that impulse!

I had no difficulty finding the garage to which I had been directed. It was the first building I reached, stretching about five hundred feet beside the highway and correspondingly deep. As I rolled up to it I glimpsed rank upon rank of vehicles within—tanks like those I had seen at Roton, enclosed vans, platform trucks, six- and eight-wheeled trailers, all painted a distinctive, vivid green. A number of green-uniformed guards lounged in front of the structure; hard-faced individuals whose big hands were never far from their holstered guns. There was an electric feeling of tensity about the place, a brooding expectancy. But it left untouched the overalled attendant who slouched up to meet me.

He seemed of a different race. He was painfully thin, lax-jawed and dull-eyed, cut from the same pattern as the lout whose sodden indifference to his brother's terrible fate had appalled me more than his mother's agony. They were typical of the natives of this region, I found—an inbred, moronic species hardly fit for the most unexacting of common labor, dregs of humanity. The man regarded me bovinely.

"I'm Stanley Sutton," I said. "I was told to bring this car here."

"Yeh. Yer ter wait."

"For whom? How long?"

"Dunno." The infinitesimal motion of his knife-blade shoulders might have been a shrug. "Mister Mowrer 'phoned ter tell yer ter wait."

"Who's Mowrer?"

"Unh?"

"Who is this Mowrer?" I repeated, slowly and distinctly.

"Boss's secatary."

There was evidently nothing to be gotten out of the creature. I slid out of the car to stretch my legs. The guards had clotted in a knot, were pretending elaborate unconcern, but I knew, as one does know those things, that I was the subject of their low talk, their furtive inspection. This was natural enough; I was destined to assume a rather important place in the community. Yet there was something other than appraisement in the one or two glances I managed to intercept, something very like compassion, it seemed to me. Nonsense! Why should anyone pity me when I had just been given a position men of twice my age might well envy?

A distant thrumming came to my ears, rose swiftly to a booming roar. From a side road a long-hooded, black Lancia thundered up, halted in a cloud of dust. Its door flung open and Thorndal popped out.

"Sutton!" he bellowed. "Glad you're here!" His big hand engulfed mine. "Waiting long?"

"Just arrived." I am no mean height, yet his massive, iron-gray head loomed above me. There was physical power in the spread of his shoulders, the hugeness of his frame; and his face, sculptured in broad, powerful strokes, was eloquent of a mental strength that explained in some part his swift conquest of an industry that was the stamping-ground of financial giants. Just now his countenance was lined with weariness, the hard glitter of his brown eyes was somewhat dulled, but the dominant virility of the man still showed through like the luminance of an inward blaze. Somehow, other men faded in Andrew Thorndal's presence like a candle in the glare of a thousand-watt airport lamp.

"Get your bag and get in!" The moment of greeting past, he was brusque, commanding. "Snap into it."

HIS big car was filmed with the dust and mud of a long journey. Thorndal slid under the wheel. I evinced no surprise at this; one didn't expect this man to be driven by a chauffeur. The Lancia leaped into motion.

"Pleasant trip?" asked Thorndal.

"Good enough." We were purring along Newville's Main Street; as we passed there was a perceptible tightening in the bearing of the few men on the narrow sidewalk, even of the shambling, vacant-faced natives. I could see no women.

"Can't say the same. Roads were rotten from Akron. Had to straighten something out there and the damn fools kept me longer that I expected. But this car's good for a hundred or more when she's pushed, so I was able to meet you as I planned."

"I rather imagined I was to put up in town," I said.

"No. You'll stay at the house."

Newville's trim houses dropped behind and the road was bordered by trees that arched overhead and made out path a tunnel of blackness.

"I want you where I can watch you," he added. "You might get notions."

He smiled without humor, and once again I felt as if the coils of a web were tightening around me. All these elaborate precautions must be intended to conceal something more than a mere secret process. . . .

And then an uneasy question obtruded itself. Jimmy Haynes, my classmate at Tech and my predecessor here, was of course acquainted with all I was about to learn, all that Thorndal was going to such elaborate lengths to prevent me from communicating to the outside world. How had the manufacturer made certain of Haynes' silence? I realized now that no one had heard from the little man since he had gone, as I was going, to assume charge of the plant at Newville. *Where was he now?*

Something nicked the outer edge of the Lancia's beam, was revealed as a man in the center of the road, waving in a signal to stop. Thorndal grunted, but did not slow. The car hurtled at the figure. . . .

"Look out!" I yelled. "You'll hit—" But at the last instant of catastrophe the man leaped aside; we flicked by. Something thudded against the tonneau side and glass crashed. "Good God," I jerked out. "You almost killed him!"

My employer's mouth was a straight, cruel slash. "His fault," he said. "No business getting in my way."

"But you can't—" I caught myself.

Thorndal's voice was a low growl. "Can't what?"

"You can't kill a man for getting in your path."

"I can't, eh? I wouldn't advise you to try it." His eyes were smoldering. "You might as well learn right now, young man, that getting in Andrew Thorndal's way is dangerous. Especially in Newville."

I didn't answer that. What could I say? I didn't want to talk anyway. Something beside the callous ruthlessness of my chief was making the pit of my stomach squirm.

For the second time in an hour I had seen a man from whose face the blackened flesh was sloughing in rotten decay, baring the quivering, raw muscles beneath. And there had been no covering at all on his waving hand, only gray sinews lacing skeleton fingers!

A red light showed ahead; the Lancia skidded, stopped. I saw two guards advancing, and behind them a high fence of copper wire in parallel strands. It came out from the right, crossed the road and disappeared to the left. But it was the square white sign hanging from it, man-high, that caught my eye. The letters on it were a staring red:

> DANGER
> This fence is
> ELECTRICALLY CHARGED
> It is
> DEATH
> TO TOUCH IT

"Evening, Mr. Thorndal," one of the uniformed men was saying. "I'll have the current off in a minute. Had any trouble on the way up?"

The magnate's voice was sharp. "Why? Expect any?"

The fellow shuffled his feet uneasily. "No, sir. Only there's been someone hangin' around in the woods off there, and a couple stones were thrown at Miss Thorndal's car when she came in last night."

"What? What's that? Nan here?" There was no doubt about it, consternation was vibrant in his tones. "How did she pass the outer lines?"

"I—I dunno. Guess they didn't dare stop her."

"Look here," snapped Thorndal, "the orders are that no one gets in without a pass. No one, do you understand, my daughter or the devil himself. Tell Captain Daley that. No! Tell him to call me at once. I'll flay the hide off him."

The man saluted, awkwardly. "Yes sir. I'll pass the word." The tiny red light at the top of the fence blinked out. "Power's off, sir." I thought there was resentment in the guard's eyes, but his

swarthy face was masklike. A panel opened in the fence, gatelike, and gears clashed.

"The brat," Thorndal muttered to himself. "I told her to stay away from here! Well, she'll go back in the morning or I'll know the reason why."

CHAPTER THREE

God of Vengeance

GRAVEL crunched under our wheels. I was aware of a house ahead, of windows warmly lighted. We rolled to a stop, a door opened at the head of a short flight of stone steps, and a man came out. Despite his livery he shambled down the stairs, his long arms lax at his side, and there was something queerly robot-like in his movements.

"Take Mr. Sutton's bag to the room Haynes had," Thorndal snapped. Then he turned to me. "Come on in, Sutton, and I'll introduce you to your new quarters." I thought the weariness in his face had deepened in the last few minutes. Certainly there was a hint of worry in his eyes.

There was a priceless Ispahan on the floor of the entrance hall, something baronial in the lift of the curving staircase toward the rear. I thought of the hovel back on the road, where a faceless man lay dying. A door to one side opened and someone came out, peering through thick spectacles.

"Hah, Mowrer!" Thorndal rumbled. "Got those papers ready?"

The secretary was a gray little man, bent and shriveled. "Yes, Mr. Thorndal," he answered. "They are on your desk. Glad to see you back safely. Were you . . . Did they . . ."

"No. I couldn't do anything with those imbeciles. They insist there has been absolutely no change in the composition they're using on the suits. By the way, this is Stanley Sutton, our new superintendent. My secretary, Carl Mowrer."

Mowrer mumbled some sort of acknowledgment of the introduction, turned back to his superior. "Johnson reports ten additional laborers incapacitated, sir," he said. "And there's three died today."

Thorndal's face hardened. "The devil! That means more slowing up of production while they break in new hands."

"It is annoying, sir." Was I mistaken, or was there a faint hint of irony in the little man's bland voice? "Hampden is waiting in the study to see you. I told him you would be too tired for business tonight, but he insisted. Said he had something you would want to hear about immediately. Shall I tell him to come back in the morning?"

"No. I'll talk to him now. Take care of Sutton for a minute." The manufacturer wheeled eagerly to the door from which Mowrer had come, slammed it shut behind him.

The secretary sighed, and turned to me. His jaw jerked sidewise. "So you've come to take Jim Haynes' place, eh . . . You're not afraid?"

"Afraid?" I echoed wonderingly. "Of what?"

"Of him and his devil's brew. Hasn't he told you how Neosite is made?"

"No. He's told me nothing."

The fellow's gnarled fingers twined nervously with one another. He moved closer to me and peered up into my face. "You're young," he muttered. "Too young. Go away. Go away before he tells you. He'll let you go now. He won't after you know. You'll want to run to the end of the world. But it will be too late then. Too late!" Suddenly he was laughing, soundlessly but horrible. "Too late!"

I grabbed his thin arm, dug my fingers into it. "For the love of Peter," I gritted.

"What's this all about? What's going on here?"

"Mowrer!" It was Thorndal's voice from the study door, but brittle, menacing as I had never hear it. "Come here." He had an opened letter in his hand and his face was livid with repressed rage. "Yes sir." The old man's eyes were fixed on the letter Thorndal held. Suddenly his cheeks were the color of death. "What is it, sir?"

"Did you write this?" He thrust it at Mowrer. "Did you?"

"Where—how—"

"How did I get it? What do you think I pay Hampden for? Did you think he wouldn't know that you gave it to a truck-driver to mail in Roton?"

"Yes—yes sir."

"Well, you have another think coming. So it was you, not Haynes, that Tri-State Oil was dickering with!"

The man made a little helpless gesture.

"You were going to sell me out for a hundred thousand, and they were willing. But they balked at sending a plane in to get you out." Thorndal's voice rumbled lower and lower, till it was like nothing so much as a volcano about to erupt. Mowrer was almost groveling before him. "Speak up! I want you to admit it with your own lips."

"It—it was the only way I could escape from here. And I had to get away—" his voice rose shrilly—"before I went completely mad. I had to get away from this hell . . ."

Did Thorndal flinch, infinitesmally? You couldn't tell it from the deep, deadly murmur of his tone, as he said: "You'll taste real hell, Mowrer, now. They need men in the nitration room. Go to Johnson and tell him I said you were to work there."

I felt let down. All this to-do, and then a mere demotion! What . . .

Then Mowrer shrieked, "Not that! Oh

God! Not that! Jail me! Kill me! But don't send me there!" His lips were absolutely colorless, his eyes stared horror. He dropped to the floor and squirmed to Thorndal's feet. "Don't make me work in there!"

THE tycoon shoved him away with a heavy shoe. "You should have thought of that before you tried to doublecross me." His face was granite, his eyes contemptuous. "You'll go into that room tonight, and if you make any more fuss you'll go without a suit."

"Without a suit . . ." Suddenly, so quickly I did not see how he managed it, Mowrer surged to his feet, was swarming, an infuriated midget, over Thorndal's huge frame, his clawed hands scoring scarlet furrows across the magnate's cheek. The big man staggered under the unexpectedness of the onslaught, tore blindly at the whirlpool of mad fury the other had become. I heard a maniacal, snarling whimper, saw Mowrer's nails go for the big man's eyes. I saw a knife flash in his other hand. And sprang.

I grabbed, caught the knife wrist, jerked it back till the little man screamed in agony, got an arm around his neck and clamped it tight. Mowrer's feet lashed out, struck Thorndal square in the belly —and then I had ripped the maddened man away from his astounded victim. I tripped, stumbled backward, crashed to the floor with the mewling, screaming fellow atop me.

A whistle shrilled, and I was threshing about the floor, scarcely able to hold the armful of explosive energy terror had made of the meek, near-sighted clerk, fighting to keep the gleaming knife out of my flesh, the clashing teeth from my skin. The tramp of heavy feet was all about me. I saw green uniforms, felt Mowrer ripped from my hold, and I lay gasping, exhausted.

Thorndal was dabbing a white handkerchief at his scratched face. Little lights crawled in his dark eyes, but there was no expression on his countenance save two white spots that came and went on either side of his nostrils. The secretary was limp in the grasp of two burly guards.

"Take him to the nitration room," Thorndal said grimly. "And tell Johnson he is to work without a suit."

Mowrer lifted his head. He had lost his glasses in the struggle, his pupils were tiny, the whites of his eyes bloodshot. But there was no fear in those blurred orbs. Hate peered from them, hate and an awful threat. Words dripped from his twisted mouth. . . .

"There is a God, Thorndal, a God of Vengeance," he said. "He knows what you do, and prepares His punishment. Even the least of His creatures may be His instrument to that end. Even I." Then his look dropped to me.

"And you, poor fool," he said. "You have made your choice. I shall not forget you when the time comes. Pray, if you can, for you are doubly doomed."

"Take him away," Thorndal gestured imperatively. Mowrer went steadily toward the door, proudly erect between his captors. Torn, bleeding, disheveled, he dwarfted us all in that moment. The hatchet-faced manservant let them out.

I got to my feet, painfully. Thorndal stared at me, for a moment, as if he were seeing me for the first time. Then he spoke:

"I'm glad you saw that, Sutton. You'll know better than to try to fool me now."

FOOTSTEPS sounded overhead.
"Dad. Daddy! What's happened?" I twisted to the flute-like voice from the stairhead. "What was all that noise?" The girl came running down the stairs,

filmy draperies streaming out behind her, white face anxious. I saw full-curved, red lips, great lustrous eyes, a coif of ebony hair. "Ohhh, you're bleeding!"

"Nan!" There was a throaty tenderness in his ejaculation. He held his arms out to her and she nestled within them.

"But Dad—that's an awful scratch—"

"Never mind that." He pushed her away from him but still held a tight grip on both her arms, just above the elbow. It seemed to me his glance drank her in thirstily. Then suddenly his face was granite once more, his eyes hard. "Why did you come here, Nan? You know I forbade you to."

It was the gruffness of his tone, rather than the words, I thought, that brought the hurt look to her face. "I know. But I was lonesome for you, and Bill Lannon was motoring up this way. So I came along. He's upstairs. You'll like him."

The white spots of rage were visible again, at the outcurve of his nostrils. "You brought someone here." He said it slowly, icily.

She was petulant now, in the way girls have when trying to avoid the consequences of a transgression. "But Daddy, he's swell," she said. She half-turned, and called, "Billy . . . oh, Billy. Come down and meet my father."

"Coming."

He was a typical playboy, the fellow who rattled down the staircase, meticulously dressed, his little blond mustache waxed, his hair slicked back. His round face was insipid, his blue eyes insolent. He reached the lower floor, halted.

"This is Bill Lannon, Dad," said the girl. "Isn't he nice?"

Thorndal grunted. Lannon bowed. "I have been very anxious to make your acquaintance, sir," he said. "Nan's father, I was sure, must be exceptional."

That to the man who had swept like a meteor across industry's sky! Could the chap possibly be so arrant an ass? He looked at the girl fatuously, and I knew I disliked him heartily. But I didn't realize, then, why I did.

"Thanks." Dryly. "I hope you find the sight worth a long trip for a short stay. A very short stay . . . Nan is leaving here at once, and you also."

The chap looked bewildered. But Nan flashed around to her father with something of his own spirit. "Dad," she said. "You can't do that! You can't chase us out the minute we've gotten here."

Thorndal's mouth was grim, but I fancied there was anxiety mixed with the smouldering wrath in his eyes, as he answered. "I can't have you stay here, Nan, not even one night. There's something—I am too busy. And you know I don't allow visitors in Newville."

"I know. I shouldn't have come. But you're not going to send me right away. Without even a chance for one little chat with you, Daddy . . ."

He weakened. "All right. You may stay overnight, with the understanding that neither of you is to set foot outside this house."

THE girl's lips firmed, but she knew when not to press an advantage. "All right, Dad. I won't go outside tonight and I won't let Bill." I noticed she said nothing about the morning. "We'll just sit around the fire in my sitting-room and talk. Come on up."

"Not now," he said. "I must go over matters with Mr. Sutton, my new superintendent." She looked at me for the first time, coolly. My heart skipped a beat. "We have lots to do before I can rest."

"I'm Nan Thorndal, Mr. Sutton," she said then. "I was wondering how soon Dad would see fit to introduce us."

I muttered something, I'll be hanged if I know what. She rattled on. "You must join us after you're through. Mr. Haynes and I were great pals till dad exiled me to Florida a month ago."

"We were classmates at Tech," I told her. "But he kept away from the rest of us. Sensitive about his appearance, I imagine."

"He did look rather like a queer old gnome, with his tremendous head and shriveled-up little body. But how could he have been your classmate? He must have been forty-five at least."

"No. He was no older than thirty."

"Come on, Sutton," Thorndal interrupted. "Let's get to work. You two run along."

He watched them scurry up the stairs, and his mouth twisted. I don't think he realized that he spoke aloud. "I'd give ten years of my life if she weren't here."

From somewhere outside there was a shriek, muffled shouts, the dull thud of a shot. Thorndal hurtled to the outer door, slammed it open and lunged out into the night. I followed.

A hundred yards away, across a sloping lawn, a line of red lights marked the fence, and I could see slumped forms in a dark knot just beneath one of them. As I dashed after my employer's running form an excited murmur came from the group, a shocked oath.

There was something hanging from the wire, a quivering shape outlined by a faint blue haze of electricity. My scalp tightened and my throat was dry. The shredded face seemed to be grinning at me through black lips, and the hand that was clamped to an upper wire was nothing but muscles and bones. It was the man Thorndal had tried to run down. Fire smouldered in the tattered jacket that covered the twisted torso of the tortured corpse. I sickened, then looked again. The man had an enormous head, and his body was shriveled, tiny.

I moved further away from the lethal barrier as the ground seemed to heave under my feet. Could there be anyone else with precisely the deformity that Jim Hayne's had? Anyone else with that gnome-like shape?

My employer's voice was devoid of emotion. "What happened here, Lansio?"

One of the men in green uniforms who stood on the other side of the fence answered him: "I see him come out from the woods. He got knife in hand. I holler. He no answer. Holler 'gain. He start running. I shoot, get him in leg. He fall 'gainst wire. That all."

The red lights were gone, suddenly, and the body slumped to the ground, horribly. Someone pulled it away and the lights came on again. Thorndal turned on his heel. "We'll never get through at this rate," he grumbled. It seemed to me he was watching my face, speculatively.

"What was it the woman had shrieked after me, back on the road to Newville? "I hope yer mother has to look at yer a month from terday."

I tried to say something, but the words stuck in my throat. I wanted to tell him I was going away from there. He could have his job. But that would mean I should never see Nan Thorndal again.

I followed Andrew Thorndal into the house, into his study, sat down in the chair he indicated and watched while he got paper from a drawer, adjusted an automatic pencil. And all the time I was thinking of Mowrer's warning: "*After he tells you it will be too late.*"

CHAPTER FOUR

"I am the Law!"

I LISTENED to Thorndal's voice, flowing on and on, and watched his busy pencil jot down chemical equation after equation. There seemed nothing particularly intricate about the synthesis of Neosite so far, nothing that any ordinarily skilled chemist might not deduce from an analysis of the product itself. What was the dread secret?

"From here," he rumbled, "the liquid is piped to the nitration room. This is where my new technique comes in. As the nitric acid is poured in I also add one-tenth of a per cent of—" He named a certain organic compound. "The resultant reaction is this, rather unexpectedly." Letters and symbols formed a new line on the scribbled sheet.

I emitted a low whistle and pointed to a cabalistic inscription. "I've never run across this gas." It was a by-product. "But from its formula I should judge it to be extremely caustic."

"It is. The fumes that fill the nitration room dissolve flesh like water does salt."

"You take no chances, of course. The nitration is performed in an auto clave."

He looked at me rather queerly, I thought. "No," he answered.

My skin crawled. "Then how do you guard your laborers?"

"By suits and masks made from a special rubber compound I have devised. They are fairly efficient."

"Fairly!" I was trying to match the unemotional steadiness of his tone. "Not perfectly!"

"No. We have had occasional failures. In the past two weeks they have grown in number, inexplicably. That's why I went to Akron. I thought the trouble lay in the manufacture of the suits. But it isn't there." There was just the slightest trace of cloudiness in his eyes. "We've lost twenty men from the nitration room in the past fortnight. Breaking in new ones is hampering production."

"Twenty men!" I couldn't keep the horror out of my voice any longer. "Good God—they must die horribly!"

"They do." He said it with an utter lack of expression, but his eyes were smouldering coals. "I'm afraid that stupid as are the people around here they will soon refuse to work for us, even with increased pay."

I pushed against the tabletop with my hands, pushed myself to my feet. "Look here, Mr. Thorndal," I gritted through cold lips, "I may need the money and the job you've offered me. But I can't be mixed up in this. I'm resigning."

His mouth twisted. "Not any more, young fellow. You know too much. You're going to stay here and work for me—as superintendent or in the nitration room alongside Mowrer."

There was sodden, brooding silence in the sombre room. His head lifted slightly, so that his agate eyes held mine, and his mouth was a hard, straight line. I thought of the armed guards outside, the death-dealing wires.

"All right," I said. "I'll continue as superintendent." After a while his vigilance might relax, I might see a chance to get away. "But I shall try to find a way to protect the workers."

The corners of his lips lifted in a satiric smile. "Try. But make damn sure you don't make it cost more than the expense of the labor turnover if you want me to adopt it. I won't raise the price of Neosite, and I won't cut my profit."

I shrugged. "After all, there isn't a bridge or a skyscraper built without a couple of deaths. There are fatal accidents in every factory." I must make him believe I had capitulated without reservations. "It is the price of progress."

"Now you're talking," Thorndal exclaimed, and there was satisfaction in his tone. "Sit down and we'll go on with our work."

I was searching for a weak point in the defenses, a loophole through which I might escape. And I found it!

The basic material of Neosite was crude oil, brought into the plant by pipeline from

Pennsylvania fields. The huge underground tube was indicated clearly on the maps. But there was another similar but fainter tracing, angling off to the south.

"Another pipeline," he explained. "For emergencies. It connects up with the Texas tube. It's empty, never been used."

I talked about something else, disinterestedly. But my pulses throbbed. There was the road to freedom! I noted carefully that its entrance was just below a window of the nitration room.

At last we were finished. Thorndal looked at his watch. "Three a. m., by George!" he said. "I'll show you your room." Upstairs, he added: "If you get any ideas during the night, remember Mowrer." He opened a door at the other end of the hall and disappeared.

ENOUGH illumination came in from outside for me to undress, and I didn't switch on the light in the room. My pajamas were folded across the pillow; I got into them mechanically and stretched out. I was dog-tired, physically and mentally, but I could not sleep.

I closed my eyes, and Nan Thorndal drifted across my imagining, her white grace in poignant contrast to all the horrors I had seen, gayety and fervor for living dancing in her eyes.

The loathesome triangle of a snake's head rose behind her, peered over her shoulder. I saw its forked tongue darting, saw that it was poised to strike. It hissed warningly. Its eyes were like Thorndal's, glittering hard . . . The hissing grew louder—I tried to yell a warning to the girl—and woke trembling.

But the hissing continued, low, insistent. It was somewhere in the room. There was a faint odor too, rank, pungent, like the unfamiliar stench in the hut where 'Lije lay dying. It had grown darker; the ceiling was only a faint, pale glimmer. I forced my head around, against the paralysis of inexplicable fear that held me—forced it around to the seeming source of the sibilant noise. And saw a green-glowing mist billowing along the floor!

It came from the gloom of the further corner, a thin veil of iridescence rolling ominously, its advancing edge sharply defined. It was coming swiftly toward my bed. Before I could gather my sleep-bemused faculties and guess its meaning, the ominous tide was lapping at the legs of my couch, was reaching tenuous, hungry filaments up toward me.

A sound at my door—someone breathing heavily—snapped the spell that gripped me. I gathered myself—launched myself in a flying leap that sent me almost to the exit. In the instant it took for me to grasp the doorknob and get the portal open, my bare feet were immersed ankle-deep in the green vapor. Then I was through, had crashed the door behind me and leaned, gasping, against the wall. Agony seared my feet where they had dipped into the gas, the excruciating torture of a burn from boiling acid.

Something squttered to my right. I twisted, saw someone flick down the curving stairs. I had only a glimpse of him in the wan light of the single burning lamp. I shouted something unintelligible, started after him—and whirled to the boom of Thorndal's voice. "Sutton!"

He was gigantic in the dimness, and he was much too near to have come all the way from his room since I had slammed the door! Red rage exploded in my skull.

"You devil," I squeezed out through a tightened throat. "What are you trying to do—kill me in my sleep?" I took a step toward him, my hands fisting, and stopped as pain shot up my legs from my scorched feet. The pain was growing worse.

His face was a frozen mask, but there was a red glow in his eyes. "What do you mean?" he rumbled, speaking low. "What's going on here?"

Doors were opening along the hall. "You know damn well what I mean," I snapped. "The gas in my room—if I hadn't wakened in time I'd be dead!"

Behind him Nan came out into the hall, a pastel-shaded negligee tightly clasped around her exquisite form. She was sleepy-eyed, pale.

"Gas in your room." There was no surprise in his calm voice.

"Yes. The green hell-gas. Look!" I lifted one foot. Already the skin was black. It was like a skin-tight shoe.

"Get in there and wash it off!" He jerked a thumb at a bathroom door, just across from my bedchamber. "Use plenty of soap. If you've had only a touch that will stop it. Hurry!" The impact of his authoritative command, my terror that in moments the flesh would peel from my extremities, drove anger from me. I dove into the room he indicated, snapped on the light and twisted bathtub spigots in frantic haste. But I left the door open, listened and watched as I flinched from the sting of the soap I had snatched up.

"Dad." Nan asked. "What . . .?"

"Nothing, dear. Just an accident. Sutton was fooling with something Haynes left in there and burned himself. Go back."

"But—but I'm frightened, Dad. I want to stay with you."

"Please go to your room." His voice was commanding, but his eyes devoured her. The outer skin was peeling from my feet and ankles as I rubbed the lather in, and the soap burned like fire. "You will be in the way here," he said. "I'll come to you later. Go, please."

SHE sighed, vanished. Lannon came into sight, in orchid pajamas. Not a hair was out of place on his head or in that tiny, pointed mustache of his. But

his insipid face was colorless, and he clutched a pearl-handled pistol in one white hand. "Is anything wrong?"

The big man ignored him. He was looking at the floor, at the threshold of the room I had quitted in such haste. I swung my legs out of the tub, reached for a jar of cold-cream. The burning was gone from my feet and ankles, but they were raw, tender. The salve relieved the pain somewhat, and I stood up gingerly, peered to see what it was Thorndal watched.

Along the lower edge of the door green smoke was seeping out.

Thorndal's head lifted. "That's got to be shut off or it will fill the house. Here you—" He turned to address someone beyond my vision "Go in and see what you can do.

I hobbled out of the bathroom and looked to see whom he was ordering into that death-filled room, that chamber of horror. It was the robot-like servant, uniform trousers hastily pulled on over a drab, grimy union-suit in which he evidently slept. The man shambled forward as I came out, his vacuous eyes fixed on his master's. Was it ignorance or mechanical obedience that was sending him unprotesting to terrible death?

"My God!" I ripped out. "You can't let him go in there. The room must be filled with the stuff by now. Why, it's murder!"

Lannon's jaw was dropped, his mouth gaped stupidly. Thorndal looked at me and his gaze was basilisk. "Keep out of this, Sutton," he said icily.

The man's hand was on the door-knob, but my cry seemed to have penetrated his dull intellect. He said, fumblingly: "Is it the Peelin' gas, boss? I don't know as I want ter go in." There was something pathetic in his irresolution. Evidently defiance of Thorndal's orders was quite beyond his conception.

"Go in and turn it off," the latter

snarled, and jerked the door open. The ominous hissing flashed out, and the room was fogged with the green haze of death. "See it?" Thorndal shouted. "A drum in the corner." His big hand struck Jever's back, thrust him in. The door slammed behind the man, and a muffled scream sounded from within—a scream of anguish. I thought I heard stumbling footsteps going across the floor. Then there was the thud of a falling body.

Thorndal's ear was against the panel. "The hissing's stopped," he said. "He shut it off before he dropped."

"Good Lord," I yammered. "It's murder. Murder!"

The other's eyes were bleak. "Not murder, Sutton. Justice. Someone had to cut the gas off or we'd all be killed. Jevers could be spared the best. And besides he had it coming to him. He helped Mowrer get his double-crossing messages out."

My pulses hammered. "You have no right to take the law into your hands!" If it meant that I would meet the same fate I had to say it. "You—"

"I *am* the law in Newville. Get that fixed in your mind, young man. *I am the law.*"

With an effort I shrugged and turned away. If I ever got out of here alive I would show him there was another law, stronger than his.

Thorndal's voice broke in upon my thoughts. "Where's that nincompoop Lannon?" he asked.

"He was here a minute ago," I answered heavily. "Right here."

"I want to tell him—"

A room door had opened; the playboy bustled out. He had gotten into clothes, and he had a heavy bag in his fist. His cheeks were the color of putty.

"Hey, you! Where do you think you're going?" growled Thorndal.

"Away. I'm going away from here."

Thorndal moved toward him ominously. "Oh, no, you're not," he said grimly. "You're staying right here. You've seen too much."

Hysteria leaped into Lannon's voice; I swear there were tears in his eyes. "Don't touch me," he quavered. "Keep your hands off me!"

"I wouldn't touch you with a ten-foot pole. But if you're looking for trouble just put a foot outside this house. You'll get it."

"Good Heavens!" The bag dropped from his nerveless fingers. "I should never have come here."

"That's the first sensible thing you've said," Thorndal commented dryly. "Now, get back in your room and stay there."

CHAPTER FIVE

The Living Dead

THROBBING pain rendered sleep impossible, and I sat in the new room I had been given, my feet on a pillow and my chin cupped in a hand whose elbow rested on the windowsill. The sky had cleared, and below my vantage point the lawn sloped, moonlit, to the circling line of red pin-points marking the electrically-charged fence that had already taken a life that night.

Somewhere a clock struck four. Two hours to daylight yet. Three hours till I should have to go into that factory where horror stalked—till I should have to face Andrew Thorndal again.

For I knew now that it was a battle to the death between us. I must smash him, smash his fiendish mill—or die. As long as his power remained I was a prisoner, a slave, sending other helpless slaves to incredible tortures.

What kind of man was he? Incredibly hard, ruthless, murderous. And yet he was sane. In all his long exposition of the intricate manufacture of Neosite, in the hours that I had studied him, there had been no hint of anything to the contrary. He was no madman, but merely one utterly without human feeling, driving straight to his objective of the production of his motor fuel cheaply and in quantity, without regard to what sacrifice that objective entailed.

And when he discovered a spy, a traitor, he sent him to death as spies and traitors are sent to death in war—utterly without compunction.

My brow knitted. All this seemed logical—devilishly logical. But why had he tried to kill me with gas hidden in my room? That was not like him. If he trusted me, there was no reason for such an attempt. If he did not, he would not hesitate to shoot me down like a dog—or send me to the nitration room. I was utterly in his power. There was no need for deception, for the planting of an opened drum where it would take me in my sleep.

He had not bothered to deny my accusation. But somehow I could not believe him guilty of that abomination. *Someone else had tried to kill me!* Who, and why? *Would he try again?*

My scalp tightened. The struggle against Thorndal that had been forced on me was alone a titantic task. What could I do against another enemy, unknown, striking at me invisibly from the night?

At this unpleasant point in the whirligig of my tired mind I became conscious of a furtive murmur, voices too low to be intelligible. This was curious!

I looked along the house-side, and saw that someone was squatted on the slanting verandah roof, two windows away.

Could it be that the secret enemy was lurking in that chamber, unknown even to Thorndal? It would have been easy enough to steal along the slanting boards and slip a tank of gas into the room where I had been sleeping. Holy Moses! Maybe it had not been intended for me at all; perhaps it had been meant for Thorndal himself. No—he slept at the end of the hall; no possibility of a mistake. For Nan, then! My blood curdled. Perhaps the plotters were planning even now to rectify their error!

The man on the roof moved, just then, and slid over its edge. He was a shadow flitting across the lawn. A patch of moonlight caught him, momentarily, and I saw that he was tall, painfully thin, his hatless head a high, hairless dome. He went into shadow again, and vanished.

And then I saw something that drove the puzzle from my mind. The long arc of red lights blinked out! Dim forms appeared suddenly from the black cluster of the bordering woods, all along the fence, and suddenly there were silent, shadowy struggles everywhere. Not one of the surprised guards had time to shout or shoot. Even at this distance I sensed the venomous quality of those struggles.

Almost before I realized they had begun they were over, and a swarm of dark, distorted forms were climbing the wire barrier that was no longer impregnable. They were running across the lawn, queer distorted shapes, more fearful for the silence of their coming. The foremost reached the swath of moonlight and I saw that he was Mowrer, had Mowrer's slight figure at least, though the face I glimpsed was as black as coal, black as my feet had been after an instant's contact with the green gas.

Thorndal's victims had risen at last, were coming to take their vengeance. Let them come! Swift elation rose in me, then vanished. Nan! What would they do to her if they won into the house? Nan!

I plunged for the door, slammed it open, and yelled, "Thorndal! Thorndal! They're coming!"

He must have slept lightly or not at

all, for he was out of his room almost before I could turn towards it. "What is it?" he snapped. "Who's coming?"

"Mowrer and a gang from the plant! They've killed the guards and—"

He had popped back through his door, was out again instantly with guns in his hands. Nan appeared, and Lannon, his blue eyes popping from his head. There was a crash from below and through the upper windows came a shrill tumult of cries, the arid yells of a bloodthirsty mob.

"Here, Sutton, take this," Thorndal shouted, and tossed a gun to me. "Watch the stairhead."

He twisted to Lannon, handed a revolver to him. "Get back in your room and guard the porch roof."

"Give me one, Dad. You know how well I can shoot." Nan was pale but calm. There was something of her father in the set of her little jaw. He looked at her, and obeyed.

"God bless you, girl! You watch the porch, too; I don't trust that milksop."

She smiled bravely, jerked open the door of her bedroom and disappeared within. The bedlam from below was terrific now; something was thudding against the entrance door in great crashes that shook the building, and there was the smash of breaking glass.

Behind me there was the sound of moving furniture. "Here, help me with this," came Thorndal's voice. He was hauling a huge chifforobe out of a room close by. I sprang to his aid and got it across the stairhead. It filled the space, would shield us well enough, while at either flank there was just sufficient space for us to see past and shoot. I crouched at one side, Thorndal at the other. And the entrance portal crashed in!

THEY poured through and filled the lower hall, a howling, shrieking mob. It was dark down there and I could see them only dimly, but the foul stench of their putrescence swept up to me, and the pungent aroma of the green gas. A black shadow leaped for the stairs and my gun spat. He fell—crashed down, and sprawled in the dimness.

"Too dark," I grunted. "Too dark down there." Gun-flash answered my shot and bullets thudded into our barricade. "I can't see to shoot."

"There's a switch here," my companion growled. "Wait."

A click, and light flooded the milling crowd. It was greeted by a volley of shots and shrill, weird yelpings that made a madhouse chorus. Thorndal's weapon thudded, but for a horrified instant I could not fire.

Down there, in that luxuriously furnished lobby, some grotesque nightmare had spilled its creatures in an affrighting, obscene throng. Not one of them was human-looking. Not one. They ranged from some who were merely blackened by the first touch of the gas, through gibbering, mad-eyed beings whose cheekbones protruded and whose lips were frayed, to the incarnate horror of the dead-alive from whom all flesh had vanished. Cheekless, noseless, earless corpses, they still jerked about in a simulation of life, with a shimmering play of exposed muscles and flickering nerves whose agony was horribly visible.

If it had not been for the thought of Nan, in that moment, I should have thrust the barricade aside and thrown down to them the man who had made them what they were, thrown him down to them and plunged after. But she was there, somewhere behind, and I could not abandon her to their vengeance. I dared not think what her fate would be.

The chifforobe was jerking under the impact of their shots. They surged on.

My finger squeezed trigger and I felt the gun jump in my hand. Flayed figures fell, twitching, on the steps. Thorndal's weapon thundered beside me, took its deadly toll. But still they came on; mouthing, grimacing figures from Hell! They càme slowly because they had to clamber over the contorted bodies of the fallen. Slowly, because my lead and Thorndal's was hurtling into them, driving them back. I saw one gaunt skeleton topple, his open mouth gurgling a scream, his tongue only a blackened stump in the dark cavity of his throat.

Where was Mowrer? He had led the charge across the lawn, but I could see him nowhere now. The question flicked across my horror-numbed brain, and then the hammer of my gun clicked on an empty shell. A raw, featureless face stared through my firing slit, its eyes twin pits of damnation. The chest rocked under the impact of the attackers, toppled. I sprang backward . . .

And from somewhere behind a shriek ripped high above the triumphant clamor of the mob. A woman's shriek. *Nan!*

I whirled, and hurtled down the long corridor, Thorndal's beserk roar ringing in my ears. I was conscious of Lannon's white face, his open mouth shouting something I did not hear, and then I was hurling myself into the room where I had seen the girl go.

The window framed struggling figures. I glimpsed Nan's flailing arms, the ex-secretary's face, black save where mad eyes rolled whitely under lashless lids. I leaped to them. Someone loomed at my side. I dodged—felt the breeze of a club that just missed my head—flung a fist at the dim-seen form. It thudded sickeningly against moist flesh. I heard weakened bone crunch, and twisted again to the window. It was open, empty. I lunged to it, thrust head and shoulders out.

"Help," Nan screamed from the roof-edge. "Dad! Bill! Help!" She was still fighting at the roof-edge, against Mowrer

and another dark, tall form. I shouted something unintelligible, lifted a leg to the sill. A shot barked—to my right. Something crashed against my skull—crashed me into oblivion.

CHAPTER SIX

Free?

I THINK the first thing of which I was conscious was the pain in my feet. It seemed as if they had been rasped with sharp files and salt rubbed into the wounds. Then the racking pain at the back of my skull obtruded itself, and the weight that lay across my chest. I opened my eyes. My sensations were still purely physical—I recall that. Thought was not yet functioning at all. There was a roar in my ears and a lurid red light was all around me. I felt warm, although I was clothed only in pajamas, and I hurt all over.

Something was digging into my back and I tried to turn over. I could not move! The blow that had knocked me out had paralyzed me. I realized that I was still on the porch roof, that something lay across me, pinning me down, that I could not stir. And that the roaring I heard, the dancing red light, and the unnatural warmth could mean only one thing. Fire! The house was on fire and I could not move!

Flames licked along the upper window-sash, just within my vision, tiny jets of yellow, and red, and lucent green. Acrid sting of smoke was in my nostrils, and heat beat at me. Glass crashed somewhere and the voice of the blaze was deafening. I smelled hair burning. My own? I turned my head toward the window and saw a red face on the sill, black flesh peeling away from it, its scant hair frizzling in the heat. Soon my hair would frizzle like that, and the fire lick across my body. What a way to die!

I had turned my head! Did that mean the paralysis was gone? I heaved up, throwing off the body that lay over me. Something clattered on the roof, a cudgel. There was a bullet wound in the back of the corpse's neck and blood still seeped from it. I was on my feet, the hot tin roofing doubling my agony. A flame licked out from the window, almost caught me. I leaped from the porch-roof, doubling my feet under me, ducking my head between my shoulders, taking the fall on my back and rolling as I had been taught in gym-class at Tech. But the impact knocked the breath from me.

I struggled erect. Every move I made was painful, the grassy stubble was a torment, my head was a gigantic, whirling globe on my shoulders. I limped toward the fence where the danger lights no longer glowed, trying to gather my incoherent thoughts. Someone had shot the fellow who had stunned me just as the cudgel fell. I had been left for dead, I was free to escape from this infernal place, from this Hell on Earth. *I was free to escape!*

I reached the fence, crawled between copper strands. A mound in the road attracted my attention and I bent to it. Shredded bits of green cloth told me what lay there had been a uniformed guard two hours ago, filled with life. I looked away quickly to save my sanity.

I stood there, swaying. I was free to escape, I told myself; but something inside me denied it. I couldn't go away from here. There was something I must do. What was it? I put out a hand to the wire to steady myself—and remembered.

Nan! Nan Thorndal! Mowrer had her, he whose eyes had glared with such hate at her father, at me. He who had led the ravening throng of the green gas's victims to their long overdue uprising, he who had proclaimed himself God's instrument for vengeance! Would his crazed mind extend that vengeance to her? Had he not left the direct attack to the others while he stole behind our defenses and snatched her from her room?

I groaned, and shuddered with cold, despite the heat-blast that rolled across the lawn from the blazing house. What was he doing to her, what unimaginable torture was he inflicting on that lissome, slender, dreamy-eyed girl? What had he done to her, where had he taken her? I looked around wildly, and saw the looming bulk of the plant, saw that most of the windows were darkened, but that four were alight, near the ground. And against their staring oblongs, dark figures moved.

I cudgeled my brain for the plans Thorndal had shown me. And cursed as I got a glimmer of what Mowrer's scheme must be. That was the nitration room, the place where the gas was born that stripped men's flesh from them and killed them too slowly. Good Lord! Had he taken her there?

I DOVE across the road, was swallowed up in the shadow, and started toward those yellow windows, calming myself to coherent thought as I forced my way through underbrush that tore at my scantily covered body and slashed my already lacerated feet. I must have traced a trail of blood through those woods, but I did not feel it then. I was racked by a greater torture, hag-ridden by the vision of Nan Thorndal in Mowrer's power, in the power of his fiendish horde. Nan Thorndal—whom I knew at last that I loved, had loved from the moment I had seen her.

What could I hope to accomplish, weaponless, almost naked, weakened by all that I had passed through? I did not know, knew only that I must get to her, get to Nan, help her or share her fate.

Dread hammered at me for speed, but I could not go fast. I was too weak, the brush too thick. So I moved slowly, and had time to think.

Mowrer might be insane, but his attack had been well worked out. The stealthy gathering of his forces in the woods, their sudden silent onslaught the instant the power was off in the wires. . . .

Hold on! How had that come about? The master switch was on the lower floor of the blazing building. That I knew from the blueprints. *Someone in the house had cut the current!* Jevers was the only servant who slept in—Thorndal had told me that—and Jevers, I realized grimly, could not have been the one. There was left, as far as I knew, myself, Thorndal and Nan, and Lannon.

Was there someone else, someone unknown even to the manufacturer? The same one, perhaps, who had planted the gas in my room? The one who had engaged in that midnight conversation with the prowler of the high-domed, bald head? Where had the latter gone, anyway—of which party was he? What had that furtive talk been about, and with whom?

A vast roaring twisted me toward the burning home, a tremendous crash. The roof had fallen in, the walls were toppling, crashed even as I looked, and the triumphant flames soared heavenward in a furious outburst, a geysering of lurid, blazing gases, of great beams exploding upward, of cascading sparks and fluttering, whirling embers. Through the split open building-side, I saw the curving staircase shatter and drop into the roaring lake of avid light, saw a body wrapped in flame swirl in that inferno, a human torch. I shuddered to think that if my coma had lasted a bare ten minutes longer my corpse too, or my still-living body,

would have been enveloped in a fiery shroud.

There was an open space between the edge of the woods and the long low building that was my goal, a space shielded from the fading glow of the ashes so that sightless dark lay there.

A grotesque, twisted shadow flitted across one luminous aperture; thin shoulders and a profile that showed no irregularity marking nose or chin. I crouched, shivering a little in the before-dawn chill.

One advantage alone I had—Mowrer's ignorance of my continued existence, his belief that I was dead.

An oath, deep-voiced, came faintly to me from within, and the intonations of a protesting feminine voice. The pall of dread lifted from me ever so slightly as I realized that Nan was still alive. But the sounds stirred me into action. I started across the clearing, moving gingerly to spare my feet and avoid untoward noise. The footing here was soft earth, a blessed relief after the torture of grassy stubble and twig-covered forest ground. My burning soles felt cool iron, and I bent to it.

GROPING blindly, I felt that a metal disk was embedded in the ground, some three feet in diameter. By sheer luck I had blundered across the manhole cover to the unused pipeline, the steel-lined tunnel I had forgotten—but that now, I realized, must make an essential part of my plan.

Weakened as I was, blinded by darkness and hampered by the necessity for avoiding noise, it was a gigantic task to move the iron plate. But at last I managed it. Then I turned once more to the nitration room windows, just beyond.

They were frosted, as I have mentioned, blocking vision. But I could hear sounds, the padding of many feet, someone speaking in a high shrill voice, the noise of pouring liquid. A hairline of brighter light along the sill showed that the window was not quite tightly shut. I bent to see if I could peer through.

And someone leaped on me from behind! An arm slid around my neck, clamped tight. A knee dug into the small of my back. "Got you!" the garroter grunted, and I could not breathe. I twisted desperately, flailing fists backward at empty air. But his grip was iron, the dig of his knee into my kidneys excruciating. "Mowrer!" he shouted. "Mowrer!"

My eyes were popping from their sockets, my lungs bursting. Dimly I knew that dark figures were crowding about me; the secretary's blackened face danced dizzily before me in the window-glow. The choking arm relaxed, but hands gripped my arms, my legs. I was lifted from the ground.

"Two birds at one throw," I heard Mowrer's gloating voice. "Grab Johnson, too, and bring him in."

"But I'm on your side." It was my captor's voice, thin-edged with hysteria. "I'm on your side, Mowrer. I caught the fellow for you."

Johnson! Where had I heard that name? Oh, yes. The one in charge of the nitration room, of Thorndal's hellhole!

"On my side!" said Mowrer. "Only because you can't help yourself. . . . You can't get past my watchers where the road bottle-necks into the swamp and you think you can escape punishment this way. Nothing doing, friend Johnson. You have a long roll of misdeeds for which to answer."

There was no way out then—except through the pipeline! Good thing I had opened that manhole! Much good it would do me now. I was done for.

"I couldn't help myself," Johnson protested. "I only obeyed orders."

"You'll obey my orders now. Mine, and His whose instrument I am." There was the exaltation of the religious fanatic in Mowrer's voice, and the cold cruelty of the triumphant oppressed! No hope for mercy there, or justice. "Take him, men."

I couldn't see what was happening in the dark, but there was the sound of a scuffle, and the wordless wail of one in mortal fear. A nightmare sound! "Gag him!" Mowrer ordered implacably. Then those holding me started to move, and I saw the dark wall of the building drifting by.

Up steps, through a huge door, a vast space, shadowy, eerie with towering tanks and weird machines, half-seen. I closed my eyes to shut out the sight of my bearers, to shut out the unholy vision of those horrible faces; more horrible now for the flare of triumph, the little crawling lights of sadistic anticipation in their lidless eyes. A door opened. They lifted me over a threshhold, and I heard the door shut again. Heard Nan scream, "Mr. Sutton. Oh God! They've caught you, too!" I forced myself to look, then.

I was in a long room, ablaze with the uncanny blue of spluttering mercury lamps. A line of iron pillars marched down the center of the loft, and there were three forms bound to the columns: Nan, her fear-distorted face staring white in the luxuriant frame of her Stygian hair; Lannon, his mustache still ludicrously pointed and immaculate against the fish-belly gray of his cheeks; and Thorndal! Lashed immovably to an iron post, helpless, his clothing was half-ripped from his great frame, there were angry red weals on his hairy torso, and blood dripped from a cut over one ear. But, he was poised, defiant, his massive head was proudly erect and his rough-sculptured features were overlaid by a brooding thunder-cloud of wrath. Lightning flickered in his eyes as he saw me.

"Tie them up!" Mowrer's command crackled in the sudden silence that followed Nan's outburst.

Skinless, dreadful hands fumbled ropes around me, pulled them ungently tight, and I sagged, unable any longer to stand, supported against the metal stake by those ropes alone. A knot of gargoylesque figures about the next column to mine disintegrated, and I had my first view of the man who had taken me and had in his turn been nabbed. Johnson, foreman of the nitration room, was the tall, high-domed individual who had crouched on the porch roof and whispered secretively to someone within the house!

CHAPTER SEVEN

Jury of the Damned!

THERE were perhaps a score of them in the long room, chattering among themselves like so many apes.

Now and then one would laugh, a cackling, lascivious laugh that sent new tremors of detestation through me. Mowrer was bent over a huge rectangular vat that spread along the farther wall of the loft, watching a great pipe gurgitate into it a flood of viscous black liquid. He was talking to someone whom I could not make out. Above him there hung from the beamed ceiling a smaller glass tank, and it was filled with an iridescent fluid that I knew to be Thorndal's secret reagent. From it a pipe dipped down and ended just over the larger tank, and the corrugated wheel of a valve was within easy hand reach.

My eyes clung to that wheel and my blood curdled, for I knew that when it was turned the contents of the tank above would pour into the black fluid—and the green gas of death would boil up to dissolve the flesh, the muscles and very bones, of any who might be in that room and unprotected! In an hour anyone immersed would be tracelessly dissolved!

My eyes sought Nan's, a wordless message passed between us. My pulse leaped, the blood hammered in my veins, and emotion surged within me—wonder that the miracle I read in her veiled glance could have occurred. Then a grinning, lipless skull passed between us and our peril was recalled to me full force. My brain raced. Was there any way in which I could kill her, swiftly, before the gas seared that young beauty?

"Enough," Mowrer spoke crisply. Someone grimaced with bared facial muscles and pulled a lever over. The stream of oil cut off with a sucking sound. I could just see the surface of the black pool, two feet below the level of the floor. It heaved like some foul prehistoric monster, and noisome colors rippled over it. Mowrer turned slowly, and the man with him. My throat contorted in a soundless shriek.

His body was shriveled, tiny; the skull, all that remained of his head, gigantic. God Almighty! I had seen him dead, hours before, clamped rigid to wires vibrant with lethal lightning, seen that deformed body alight with a blue aurora that was blasting every cell within it! And now Jimmy Haynes walked across the floor, his skeleton hand on Mowrer's arm, his sightless eyes deep pits wherein white marbles rolled!

Was the little old man, whom Thorndal had condemned, indeed the instrument of God's vengeance? Had he been infused with power to raise the dead? Was this concourse of inhuman figures a gathering of the damned, raised from the grave to visit retribution upon their slayer? The solid walls rocked around me and the floor heaved beneath my feet. . . .

There was a desk on the dais near the entrance to this corner of Hades, and two chairs had been placed behind it. Those two went directly there, Mowrer guiding the other with infinite tenderness. They sat down. There was something appalling in their slow progress, an awful threat in their grim, still faces. To my tortured vision Haynes was Beelzebub himself, the ebony-skinned Mowrer his chief disciple.

In response to a motion of the secretary's hand the others ranged themselves to one side, intent, listening. Utter silence clotted in the room. The foul odor of rotting bodies was stench in my nostrils, and the mercury lamps added the last touch of horror with their ghastly light and the huge shadows they cast across the floor. It seemed to me that vast black wings beat overhead. . . .

"Andrew Thorndal!" Mowrer's tones had lost their shrillness, the thinness that had spoken of age and pain. They had a husky quality, were hushed, though clear and penetrating, as if he were himself appalled by that which he was about to do. "Andrew Thorndal! That you may not hereafter complain you were unjustly condemned, a jury of those you have wronged will hear you. Have you anything to say?"

A N INSTANT Thorndal's nostrils flared, then he was speaking, calmly, steadily: "With what am I charged?"

"With exploiting for your private profit the people of a countryside. With condemning to torture and death men too dulled and stupid to withstand you."

"They were starving when I came, were clothed in rags. I gave them work, money with which to buy food and clothing."

The voice of the accuser was implacable. "You lured them into your power," he said. "You gave them suits that at first protected them, but when you had set up your fences of death and your cordons of armed guards so they could not escape, the suits failed. You cheapened them, to save a few paltry cents in the cost of the only defense they had against the hell-gas you devised."

"No!" The syllable blasted into the room. "No! The suits failed, but that was not my fault. They were the same. I swear to you they were the same. I do not know why they failed." I felt that he was not answering Mowrer then. He was answering something within himself, some question that had robbed him of sleep, that had clouded his eyes even when I brought the subject up in our first talk an eternity before.

Mowrer returned to the attack. "If that were so," he demanded, "why did you not shut the plant till you had determined the reason and remedied it?"

Thorndal looked at him unbelievingly. "Shut down! Why I could not do that. We could not meet the demand as it was. Tri-State Oil had their backs against the wall. Another month and they would have folded up. Neosite would have been in every car and airplane tank in America. Close and give them a chance to say the supply of Neosite was unreliable, could not be depended upon! That's what they wanted; that's why I had armed guards on the road, so they could not send their agents in to shut me down. They tried it, persistently. I had to go ahead. Had to!"

Good Lord! This general of industry, this master of men, was himself a slave, a Frankestein to the monster of his own creation! In a flash I saw it. He had given himself to the service of Neosite, and Neosite had become a Juggernaut riding down and crushing out every atom of humanity in him! He would sacrifice himself to Neosite as he had sacrificed the poor, maddened creatures around us, without the least hesitation. Somewhere deep within me was born a tiny spark of pity for the man.

But not so with Mowrer and the others. The prosecutor broke the silence with, "That is your only excuse?"

"That is all." Thorndal's brown eyes had retreated again into lethargy. Something like contempt hovered about his lip corners. "I have nothing more to say."

Mowrer half-turned to the hulk in whom I had recognized Haynes. "Andrew Thorndal has condemned himself from his own mouth. Need I say more?"

The gigantic head moved slowly in negation. Then a whisper came from its mouth, an awful sibilance of sound that was like nothing save one's imagining of a voice from beyond the grave, a voice from the fleshless lips of a skeleton dead so long that even the worms had lost interest in it. Yet the words were clear: "You have heard charge and defense. What is your will?"

And that jury of the dying, those who still could talk among that jury of the damned, roared their answer: *Guilty!* Like the yapping of wild dogs it was, like a fiends' chorus from Hell.

Haynes nodded. "Andrew Thorndal," he whispered. "You will die as they died. It is my regret that you will die more quickly."

Mowrer stopped, spoke again: "Nancy Thorndal! You have danced while men died that you might clothe yourself in silks, have given yourself to pleasure while mothers' hearts were wrung with despair that you might drink fine wines. . . ."

I shouted something, and Thorndal's voice thundered: "She knew nothing about it. Let her go, you devils!"

" 'The sins of the fathers shall be visited upon the children. . . .' "

"Jury," said Haynes. "What is your will?"

"Guilty!"

God! Even they could have spared her. I ripped curses at them, but I might have been crying in a desert for all the attention anyone paid to me.

And the inexorable voice of the judge came back from the dead, husked the sentence, "You shall die in the gas."

"Stanley Sutton!" The farcical trial went on. "You were warned and persisted. You aided Andrew Thorndal and defended him from me and from his other victims. You shot down the messengers of vengeance."

"Go to hell," I snarled. "What's the use of my saying anything?"

"—Die in the gas."

I didn't care. If Nan were to go that way I was satisfied to go with her. . . .

"Randall Johnson! You were foreman of the nitration room and sent men to their death without compunction. You sat at this desk in the only suit that functioned and watched them labor in the shadow of their doom."

THE tall man turned to his accuser. "I helped you in your plot," he said. "When nobody could get through the fence I told the guard something was wrong in here and I must see Thorndal at once. They passed me through and I shut off the current that would have held you back."

So it was he who had done that! But that did not tell why he had been engaged in a covert confab with someone else on the bedroom floor. Nor could it have been he who planted the tank of gas in my room. I wished now that I had not awakened then. At least I should not have had to watch Nan die.

Mowrer was pondering Johnson's plea. He raised his head now. "No!" he said. "We used you, but that did not win for you absolution from your sins." There was a murmur of approbation from the macabre group of listeners. "You were in our power and you thought to bribe us with your offer of aid. Your guilt is too black to be washed white by one act of repentance, if repentance there was."

Thorndal was looking at the bald man with burning eyes. If he were free, I thought, he would tear him to pieces with his bare hands.

Again the ritual of reference to the jury, the chorused "Guilty," and Haynes' eerie voice pronouncing sentence: "You will die in the gas."

Johnson sagged against his lashings, and his eyes were the orbs of death. "No," he whimpered. "I can't face it." He surged up as far as his lashings would permit and screamed, "Oh, God! Don't let them do it!"

A lank creature whose face was a red blob yelled, "Shut up, yuh´rat. Yuh held a gun on me when I wanted ter git out o' here."

Mowrer, ignoring Johnson's screams, peered near-sightedly past the four of us who had been condemned. "You, there," he said. "What is your name?"

"Wuh—William Lannon." The popinjay's jaw shook visibly as he answered.

The little man who had brought about this holocaust turned to Haynes. "I know nothing against this man," he said. "His presence here is pure accident, and he did not fire at us when we attacked the house. But he must die that God's work that we do may go unpunished by man's blundering law. We dare leave no witness."

"Gentlemen!" Lannon's voice rang out. "I won't say anything. I swear it by everything that is holy to me. I won't say anything if you let me go."

There was a momentary pause. Then Haynes projected toneless words into the room: "You swear silence as to all that has passed?"

"I swear by my dead mother's name, by my only hope of salvation." He was cringing, pleading. "No one knows that I came to Newville. No one will ever know if you will only let me out of here."

He slavered at the mouth in his eagerness.

Someone called, "Let the poor fool go! He ain't done nothin'."

Haynes considered a moment, then nodded. Mowrer pointed to one who was less burnt than the rest. "Release him," he ordered.

"No!" It was a squeal so shrill that for an instant I could not locate its source. "Stop! I'll be damned if he'll go free and leave me to suffer." Johnson was yammering those words, straining at his ropes, his bound hands clawing at his sides. "Listen to me! Listen."

"What is it?" Mowrer clipped.

"Johnson! Don't tell them!" Lannon screamed, wild-eyed. "For God's sake, don't."

"Silence!" Haynes husked. "Silence. We shall hear him."

That voice from the dead struck Lannon dumb. But his mouth remained open in a soundless scream, and the terror in his eyes was an awful thing to witness. Yes, even in that chamber of horrors there could be a greater horror: his naked soul revealed in those staring orbs. My scalp tightened as I guessed what Johnson had to tell.

That one was speaking, malevolence vibrant in his now steady tones: "His name ain't Lannon. It's Rand, Morton Rand, and he's a vice-president of Tri-State Oil."

An inarticulate roar from Thorndal blasted the man's next words, a thunder-sound of fury.

"Silence," came the command of the judge who had been dead and was now alive. "Silence!"

"He got me, no matter how," Johnson went on. "A hundred grand they paid me—to put Neosite on the fritz. A hundred grand. For that I smeared oil on the rubber safety suits, so that they'd be porous an' let the gas through. I didn't put it on my own. . . ."

"You lie, damn you. You lie!"

Lannon's shriek set off a cataclysmic tumult of poise. Thorndal's boom, "You dogs! You cowardly dogs!" Johnson: "It's the truth. I can prove it." Mowrer mouthing: "God's vengeance. God's wrath upon him." And the agonizing screams of the victims of the gas: "Kill! *Kill!!* KILL!!!"

Only I was silent, horror-stricken at the lengths to which greed could go— I, and Nan. I saw that she had fainted, her head lolling, her silk-clad body erect only by virtue of the lashings that held it to the steel column next to mine.

THEY surged down the long room toward Lannon, those men whose tortures of the damned had been his procuring—a wave of maddened fiends. I saw one, faster moving than the rest, clutch a fleshless hand in the man's blond hair, and closed my eyes lest I see him ripped limb from limb. Someone scuttered by me, and I heard Mowrer's voice: "Stop! Stop men! That death's too good for him! I claim him for the vengeance appointed by God!"

There was a scream, the spat of blows, and the sounds died away. When I looked again they were going back to their places, and Lannon—or Rand—was still bound to his post, still alive. Alive, but his face was a raw, bleeding mass, one side of his mustache had been literally torn out by its roots, his torso was bare and scored with deep, gory furrows.

The blind Haynes had not moved from his seat. He waited till they were quiet again, and then rasped out: "Go on!"

Johnson's features were twisted now with bitterness. He looked odd with that towering, hairless head of his, his long neck with the Adam's apple moving up and down as he talked. "I thought the first touch of the gas would scare the men out, or make the boss quit," he was saying. "But things went right on, an' I had to obey orders and keep on making Neosite. Last night I caught sight o' Rand drivin' up to the house, an' knew he'd come to see what was what. Afterwards he told me he'd gone to the beach where Miss Nan was and kidded her into bringing him to Newville."

"Afterwards! Then you talked to him?"

"Sure. Three times. The first was through the fence, right after the boss got home. Rand told me Thorndal had brung a new super that looked smart, wanted me to fetch him a tank o' gas so's he could scare Sutton off. . . ."

Scare me off? Murder me! Rage was cold within me as I realized the viciousness of the man. . . .

" . . . I brung it to him the second time, when the current was cut off so's they could take Jim Haynes' corpse off the wire, an' the third was when you made me go. I wanted to tip Rand off, to tell him not to fight you an' he'd be all right." Johnson had been pouring out his amazing confession in a rush of hurried words, but suddenly his voice broke into a high, venomous shrillness. "I risked my neck for the devil, but I'll be damned if I'll let him get scot-free while I die for what I've done. He's the cause of it all. He—"

"Enough! We've heard enough." Mowrer's voice was surcharged with pent fury; it was the voice of doom. "He shall not escape. 'Vengeance is mine! saith the Lord.'"

And in a dread antiphony Haynes husked the sentence, "He shall die in the gas."

If ever a man deserved death Morton Rand did. But we others . . . Nan. . . .

"Men!" I twisted to the sudden bellow from Thorndal. "Men! Listen to me!" His eyes were blazing, his face alight with inspiration. "Listen!"

There was a rustle. Someone shrilled,

"No! We've heard enough from you!" But Thorndal went on, roaring down all opposition: "Listen! The suits are good! You know it now—I knew it all the time. The suits are good and we can make Neosite safely. We can make Neosite and sweep Tri-State off the map. I'll raise your wages, I'll treble production. I'll give you pensions—build schools— Newville will be the wonder industrial city of the world!"

A hissing started, venomous. High-pitched cries from blackened lips: "No! — Stop talking.— We've had enough!— Murderer!— Torturer!— The gas— *Turn on the gas!*"

Thorndal roared on, unhearing, un-comprehending. He was mad with re-newed hope, not for his safety, not for his daughter's, but for his Neosite. . . .

"Hell! I don't want to make any money out of this. I'll give all the prof-its to the workers, run the thing for nothing! Just let me go on making it. You can't kill it! You can't kill Neosite, the best damn fuel that was ever invent-ed, the fuel of the future. It will revo-lutionize transportation if you give it a chance. Listen to me. . . ."

"Silence, Thorndal." The impact of Haynes' awful voice got through him. "Silence!"

Thorndal stopped, and for the first time there was consternation in his face, realization of defeat. Not make Neosite! He just couldn't understand it.

The whisper of doom from the dead man's lips came again. "No, Andrew Thorndal," he said. "Though it was not your fault that the suits failed, yet when they did fail you drove on despite that failure, despite the black death it brought on those over whom you cracked the whip of your will, the dumb, helpless creatures your enslaved. For this you merit the death you gave them, you and yours, you

and all your works. The sentence of the court stands."

And Mowrer's harsh accents put a pe-riod to hope: "'Vengeance is mine, saith the Lord Jehovah. Vengeance is mine!'"

CHAPTER EIGHT

The Death Wheel Turns

I WAS watching Nan with anxious eyes, praying that she would not re-vive till the gas had done its foul work. The room was clear now of that awful company. We five were alone, bound to the steel columns that were to be our stakes of martyrdom, alone save for one ghastly figure. Haynes stood with his skeleton hand on the fateful valve-wheel, Haynes who was dead already and so was not afraid to die again. He stood there, the muscles that criss-crossed his skinned head taut with some inner tension, his grotesque skull canted as though he were listening through the tiny orifices where ears had once been. What sound was he listening for, what awful sound herald-ing our doom?

Somehow I could not believe that this was the end. There was no hope, and yet my brain still struggled for some way out. And . . . inspiration flashed on me! Perhaps—now that he was alone. . . .

"Haynes!" I cried. "I'm Sutton, Stan Sutton, from Tech. Your classmate. You can't kill me, Jim Haynes!"

The figure there at the wheel started, turned toward me his black sockets where-in sightless white orbs rolled. "Who calls Jim Haynes?" he asked.

"Stanley Sutton! We've studied to-gether. Remember Prof. Carlon and the campus songs? Remember the night we licked Yale? Remember commencement and the two *cum laudes,* you and I?" Was I getting it across? Tech has a strong hold on her grads; was it strong enough to stop him? "You wouldn't blast Stan Sutton with the green gas, Jim."

His rotted teeth moved in signal that he was about to speak, and I stopped, held my breath. His voice came, that hushed, spectral voice of his that had pronounced sentence of death in the court of the damned.

"Jim Haynes is dead," it said. . . . Then the awful thing was true. . . . "Thorndal killed my brother Jim and I watched him die." I rocked back against the pillar. Once, once only, I had heard Haynes speak of a twin brother, Sam. "Now Thorndal dies, and his child, and his minions who have done his will."

Haynes—Sam Haynes—turned, and twisted the valve-wheel! The iridescent fluid gushed from the pipe-mouth in a six-inch stream, struck the black pool and spattered. Some of it reached me, wet my clothing and the rope that was wound around me. A drop hit my hand, stung. It was an organic acid, I recalled, caustic almost as the green gas it produced.

"I'm coming," Haynes squalled. "I'm coming, Jim," and plunged into the black pool, disappeared beneath its surface! He shrieked as the acid burned him, and his struggles mixed the reagent with the processed oil it would change to Neosite. As by magic the fluid cleared, turned pink, then a milky-white. I stared at the faint green mist that formed on its surface, that spread rapidly, that boiled up in manifold tiny bubbles from the depths below. The green gas was rising in a lifting tide of death.

God! It rose so slowly, so deathly slow. It would be hours, hours before it reached the level of our heads. I had shuddered at the thought of swift, searing extinction by that burning mist, but I had not envisioned the dragged out torture that was in store for us. Now the awfulness of our fate burst upon me full force. Tied, helpless to move, the green gas would creep up on our tormented frames, inch by slow inch, corroding our flesh, searing deep to bone as it rose, while still we lived, while still we were conscious of every agony, every torture of that slow advance!

THE tendrils spread, coalesced, formed a thin pool on the stone floor, a pool that rolled nearer, gradually nearer with its terrible threat. I pulled my eyes away from it, sought Nan again. She was awake! She was staring at the green gas and her eyes were pits of terror.

"Nan," I called. "Nan!" And, forgetting they were bound, I tried to raise my arms to her.

Tried to! Almighty God! They came up! The rope snapped, and my arms lifted!

I gazed at my hands unbelievingly, saw white marks of acid burns on them. The reagent that had splashed on me—the iridescent acid. . . . I glanced at the frayed rope-ends, moist and blackened. . . . The acid that had spattered on them had eaten through the thongs binding me—had freed me!

"Nan," I gibbered, laughing hysterically. "Nan, it's all right. I'm loose! Heads up, Nan!" I worked frantically at my lashings and got them off, leaped to her and liberated her. There was a long shelf under the windows, a shelf on which bottles were arrayed. I lifted her to that. "Stay there till I get the others untied," I said. She should be safe there, safe for thirty minutes at least, so slowly was the gas coming.

Thorndal was exultant as I plucked at his ropes. "Good work, Sutton," he said. "Good work! We'll get out of here and start all over again. We'll build another Neosite factory somewhere else and you shall be my partner. You'll run the plant and I'll attend to distribution."

My hands dropped away from the

knots. "Nothing doing, Thorndal. Swear to me there will be no more Neosite or I'll leave you here."

"No more Neosite! Man! You're crazy!"

"I will be crazy if I let you start making that hell's brew again."

"Hurry, Stan. Oh, hurry!" Nan called to me from her perch. "Look, the gas is near you. It will burn you and dad!"

I twisted. There it was, inches away from my feet, the burned feet whose pain I had forgotten in the blazing excitement of all that had happened. It was spreading all through the long room, but there was time yet. I turned back to Thorndal. "Well, what do you say?"

"No! I'll never promise that. If I did there would be no reason for me to continue living." He was honest, at least. He could have given me the promise I demanded, and broken it later.

"Then you'll stay here."

I turned away. And Nan screamed, "Stanley! Stanley Sutton! What are you doing? You're not going to leave my father. You're not!" She started to scramble down from her refuge.

"Get back there! Get back, I say!"

"Not unless you untie dad. If you don't, I shall."

I stared at her determined little face, so like Thorndal's now, and weakened. "All right, Nan," I answered. "Get back." I don't know whether I would have gone through with my bluff, but I had been determined to extort the promise from him. The first touch of the gas would have— But she had settled that. It took me seconds to complete the job.

"Fine," Thorndal grunted, stretching. "Get Nan away. I'll take care of the others."

"All right," I snapped. I was beginning to fear someone would come back to see why Haynes had not emerged, for surely they could not have known of his

contemplated suicide. "We're going out the window. . . ." I rattled my plan, then leaped for the shelving, thrust up the window. It screeched in its disused grooves.

IT WAS broad daylight now. I saw the round black hole from which I had removed the cover. . . . My eyes lifted, and far beyond the woods I saw figures turning to the sound of the window's opening. They started to run back, but one remained behind. I saw a rifle lift to his shoulder, saw the flash of its firing. "Come on, Nan," I gasped. "Quick."

She clung to me, frightened. "We can't get away, Stan," she said. "They'll catch us."

"Come on!" I got an arm around her, thrilling even in that instant to the warm softness of her body, and jumped. It was only a step to the opening to the oil pipe, but a bullet whistled uncomfortably close to my head as I took it, half-dragging Nan with me. Then I was kneeling, peering down into the pit. It looked dry, clean. "Down here, Nan," I said. "It's our only chance."

She hung back. "Dad. He isn't. . . ."

"He's freeing the others. He'll be right along. Hurry!" Another bullet spat dust a foot from us. "Slide in and I'll lift you down. Quick!"

She was sitting on the well-curb, her feet within. I took her hands, swung her down. Her face lifted to me, a pale oval in the dimness of the shaft. "I can't reach bottom with my feet," she told me.

"I'll drop you. It's only a foot or two." I let go, and heard her thud to the bottom. "Are you all right?"

"Yes. It's a tunnel, Stan. I can stand almost straight in it."

"I know." I looked up. The running men were nearer, and the one with the rifle was aiming more carefully.

"Is dad coming?"

I glanced back. Thorndal was heaving through the window and something metallic gleamed in his hand. I slid into the bore, hung from its rim by my hands. "Look out, Nan!" I cried, and let go.

The hole was deeper than I thought, ten feet at least, its sides smooth. The shock of my landing sent pain shooting up my legs. The light-disc above darkened and I ducked back into the conduit. Distant shouts came to me, and Thorndal dropped down the well.

"I have a gun, Sutton," he said. "It was in the lab and I knew we'd need it. Cartridges, too, this time. We can stand them off indefinitely here."

"Johnson! Lannon! Are they coming?"

"Coming?" he snarled. "Hell! That double-crosser and the hound who bought him? They won't bother us any more. They're stewing in the tank."

My mouth opened, closed. I couldn't say anything. They deserved it, but only Thorndal could have done that. My mind flashed back to the scene in the lobby when Mowrer had been dragged off to the nitration room at his command. He hadn't changed. All he had endured was powerless to change him!

Sunlight streamed down the shaft, and dust motes danced in it. Then a shadow fell blackly down.

"Keep back," Thorndal shouted. "Keep back or I'll shoot!" He backed away from the bottom of the well, crouching, the bulldog revolver snouting. . . .

There was a muffled clamor above, the shrill voices of the gas-blasted men whose doom we had escaped. The shadow flickered away, returned. And suddenly a twisted shape thudded down!

The thunder of Thorndal's gun deafened me. Nan screamed, and her father's full-chested bellow echoed in the pipe behind: "One down! Any more coming?" There was a note of triumph in his tones,

the exultant lift of a fighting man at the smell of battle. I moved back to where Nan knelt, got an arm around her. The man Thorndal had shot was a crumpled heap in the light. He rolled his flayed face toward us, the ligaments quivering. His eyes glazed, and he didn't move again. We waited, but nothing happened.

"They're licked, Sutton," Thorndal growled. "They don't dare come down. We've got them licked!"

I could distinguish Mowrer's high-pitched voice, crisp with command, and doubted Thorndal's statement. They couldn't come down to pursue us, but he would find a way to get at us. He was indomitable, implacable. He would not allow us to escape his revenge so easily. Thus my thoughts, but to Nan I whispered, "We've won, darling. We've won! They can't touch us now." The term of endearment came naturally; I had not forgotten the message of her eyes. . . .

"That horrible face!" She shuddered. "I can't stand it. Stan, it's driving me mad."

"Here. Hide your eyes against my shoulder."

CHAPTER NINE

Nightmare Flight

MINUTES dragged. The huge pipe in which we had found refuge stretched back behind us into blackness, its steel walls rusty. I knew that it stretched so for miles, till it met the pipe-line from the Texas oilfields.

"Sutton," Thorndal called, without turning his head. "About two miles back this pipe comes to the surface and lies along the top of the swamps. There's another manhole there, for cleaning purposes. You and Nan make for it, and get help from Roton. I'll hold the fort here."

"That will take hours. You can't keep vigilant forever. They'll catch you napping and grab you again; come after us. I'll stay here with you, and Nan will go for help."

She stirred in my arms, pulled away. "No!" she said. "No! I couldn't go through all that long dark alone. And besides, I won't leave dad and—and you, Stan."

"Good God, girl!" I burst out. "You must. It's the only way, the only way we'll ever get out of here."

"You go, dear." Ineffably sweet, that word on her lips. "You go. I'll watch here with dad. I can shoot."

"Ridiculous! I—"

There were ominous clinkings at the surface. "Sutton!" Thorndal exclaimed. "They're sticking a big pipe down the manhole, one of the conveyor tubes from the processing room. What do you think they're up to?"

My scalp prickled. "It's some devilment. . . . Mowrer isn't beaten yet!"

"By God! He'll be beaten before I'm through with him! Beaten to a pulp!" Thorndal banged his free hand against the steel side of the pipe in an ecstacy of defiance. "Beaten to a pulp."

"Shhh!" Nan hushed him. "What's that sound?" We fell silent, listening intently. I heard a dull throb, throb; thought it was the sound of blood in my ears. Then I was certain it was not.

"Sounds like a pump," I whispered. "But it can't be! What would they be doing with a pump?"

"I'm frightened," the girl breathed in my ear. "Stan, I'm—"

"Great Jupiter! . . . Look!"

There was a green glow, suddenly, in the aperture. We watched Thorndal's bulking frame silhouetted against it. He leaped back, cursing. I smelled an unmistakable odor. A trickle of the emerald vapor crept lazily into the thin cylinder of sunlight that still came down from the world above.

"Run!" I shouted, choking. "Run!" And even as we turned to flee the first great gush of the death-gas billowed forth to follow us! Mowrer had found a way indeed! Bullets were of no avail against the weapon he had devised to confound us!

We ran into the pitch blackness of that long tube, and the green glow of horror rolled after us, aided by the down-pitch of the tube, spurred by the throb, throb of the pump, the echoing thud of which followed us mercilessly.

I can't remember much of that nightmare flight, except that the steel was sharply curved, and its roof so close down that I was half-stooped over as I ran, that the soles of my feet were torn once more by rust and my scalp bruised again and again by some inequality overhead. Nan was somewhere in front, I next, then Thorndal—cursing, cursing in a rumbling monotone as he ran. His voice thundered as it echoed through that long tube, the pump throbbed, the green gas followed us with its deadly luminance. We stumbled onward through an infinity of lightless constricted space, an eternity of time.

How long, I thought, how long can we last? We may go on and on, but finally we must drop, and the gas will roll over us, over Nan, and Thorndal and me, and blacken our bodies as had been intended from the first.

It seemed to me I could hear Mowrer intoning his awful refrain: " 'Vengeance is mine, saith the Lord.' "

Under my tortured feet the pipe curved, slanted upward. The ascent slowed us, but it slowed the gas still more. We drew ahead of the threatening glow, and I began to hope that perhaps we should beat it. If only we were far enough ahead when we reached the manhole of which Thorndal had spoken, that we might have time to get it open before the misty death caught us!

"Faster," I gasped. "Faster, Nan!" I could barely make out the pale glimmer of her, ahead.

And suddenly she was gone! Her shrill scream echoed back to me, but I could not see her. "Stop, Stan," she cried. "Oh, stop!"

I skidded to a halt. "Nan! What's happened? Where are you?"

"Here!" Her voice came from my feet, from below me! "Here. There's a deep hole here; I slid into it. The other side's vertical. I can't get out."

"A sump hole." Thorndal was right behind me. I could feel his hot breath on my neck. "A depression to clear the oil of sediment."

I threw a fearful look over my shoulder. The gas was distant, but it rolled toward us implacably. "Watch out, Nan," I said. "I'm coming down for you."

"No, Stan. It's not far across. You and dad can jump over. Don't come down here."

I TOOK a cautious step, another. The conduit floor flattened out, slanted steeply downward. I pushed my feet over the edge, skidded, bumped into Nan's soft body. I must have fallen ten feet, at least.

"Oh, Stan! You did come! Now you can't get out, either. Feel here. ." She seized my hands, placed them against the opposite wall of the sump-hole. It was straight up and down, slick.

"All right," I grunted. "I'll lift you out."

"And you?"

"Don't worry about me. I can climb like a fly. I'll follow you."

Of course, I lied. I could get her up, but I would have to stay behind. The gas would reach here in moments, would pour over the lip of the depression and swallow me.

"I'll be all right," I assured her. "Hurry! Up on my shoulders, then grab the top and pull yourself up. Quick!" I must not give her time to think, to argue! "Up with you!" I got hands around her waist, swung her to my shoulders. She scrambled erect, I felt her heels digging into me. Then they were gone.

"I'm up, Stan. Come on."

"Go ahead, Nan; I'll be with you in a minute. Go ahead, Thorndal, jump across. It's only three feet."

"Stan! You can't get out. Oh, my dear!"

"Run, Nan, run. If you love me, run." She was safe. . . . And Thorndal could save himself. It was an easy leap.

"Watch it, Sutton," Thorndal said. Good Lord! What was he doing? Why didn't he jump? The question had scarcely framed itself in my mind when he was at my side. "Up with you, boy."

"Mr. Thorndal, you—"

"Shut up. She's my daughter and you saved her life. It should have been I. . . . It will be. Up with you—quick!"

No time for futile argument. Perhaps it was just that he should be the one to go. Rand and Johnson had paid the penalty of their crimes; why should Thorndal escape? Protesting nevertheless, I let him hoist me to his shoulders, lifted myself erect and pulled myself out of the death-trap!

I glanced back. The awful glare of the gas was close—terribly close. In seconds now it would pour down into the hole where Thorndal was.

"Nan's away," I told him. "She's safe! Maybe I can find something to help you out, maybe I can save you yet!"

"Good-bye, boy. Take good care of her. Good-bye!"

I twisted to start off.

"Stan!" It was Nan, only yards ahead.

"Stan! There's something queer here. Hurry!"

I was at her side. The roof of the pipe lifted here; I could stand up straight. I felt overhead—felt a flat plate. My pulse hammered.

"It's the manhole, Nan!" I cried. "The manhole in the swamp. We're saved! We can get out!"

"Thank God! Oh, thank God!"

I got the flats of both hands against the cover, heaved. Superhuman strength must have flowed into me then; the heavy disc lifted at once, slid sidewise. Blessed sunlight struck down!

"Up with you, Nan—up!"

I grabbed her, literally threw her out of that damned pipe. And just as I did so a scream shrilled to me, a strong man's scream. I looked back. The gas had reached the pit where Thorndal was, was folding over its edge in a lazy, slow settling of doom.

I got my hands on the manhole rim, chinned, scrambled out. The oozy, scummed surface of the swamp was Eden to my eyes. Nan had slid down the tube's surface, was ankle-deep in mud.

"Father!" Her eyes widened in sudden realization. "Where's father?"

How could I tell her? I pretended breathlessness, pretended I could not speak. The great pipe was covered with wooden slats here—bound to it by wires that were rusted by the moisture of the morass. One was right at hand.

Perhaps—my brain was working lightning fast—perhaps I could get the wire off. I jerked at it—it snapped. And I was down again in the pipe, the wire coiling after me.

The sump-hole was half-filled with green vapor when I reached it. But Thorndal—a shrieking, fear-gibbering wretch—was still alive. The wire held, I got him out, just as the gas filled the pit and eddied over its edge.

I had to guide him to the manhole, to lift his hands to the rim. I thought it was because he was numbed with fear. But when he was in the light again I saw that the eyes in his blackened face were burned white. He was blind!

* * *

Soap and hot water saved his skin. But he is a sightless, doddering old man in our home now, Nan's and mine. Our children love their grandfather, he plays with them so gently, tells such nice stories in this thin, quavering voice.

THE END

GODDESS OF EVIL

It was a wine more potent by far than any vintage mere mortals should ever know—a wine only pagan gods could drink with impunity. Yet it was the heady liquid of life to Hobart Forsythe—until it summoned to his side the beautiful and deadly Goddess of Evil Revelry. . . .

REVELRY

by Frederick C. Davis

(Author of "The Coming of the Mad Ones," etc.)

GAZE upon me and you see a normal appearing young man whose eyes yield no hint of the haunting wonder that crawls through his mind at every waking moment. It is a

only imagined her, or whether she was as actual as the wine that mothered her, I can never forget Vina.

Who was Vina? To the best of my ability I will try to tell you, but when I

Novelette of Eerie, Deadly Allure

tantalizing uncertainty that I can never solve, a question that can never be given a final answer. Yet, constantly seeking the truth that never can be revealed, I ask myself over and over: *Was she real, or a creature of dreams?*

I am speaking of the beautiful woman of the vine—of the enchanting being who appeared suddenly in the pool of wine, full-blown like a white blossom on a lake of scarlet desire. That night she came and that night she vanished. Whether I have finished you will be no surer of her than I.

I knew nothing of her, had never seen her, when darkness closed down that night. Soon after dinner I excused myself, and stole alone down into the blackness of the basement, drawn by the lure of the wine. The thirst was upon me. Secretly, soundlessly, I went through the dank gloom toward the chamber where the wine was stored in its great, ancient tun.

At the mouldered oaken door I paused. With my trembling hand on its huge, rusty latch I listened. Suspended on great, hand-wrought strap-hinges, it stood old and massive in its heavy frame, crusted with strange fungus growths that glittered crystalline in the flickering light of my candle. It was a timeless portal shut upon silence—silence disturbed only by muted voices.

Voices were speaking somewhere above me. In one of the remote rooms of the musty old dwelling two persons were talking in low, guarded tones. A woman's anxious words alternated with the grave phrases of a man. The woman, I knew, was my wife, the man my closest friend. I sensed that they were discussing me, trying to analyze the preternatural change that had come over me. Until, at last, they became quiet, I stood listening at the ancient door.

I opened it slowly. It swung ponderously into heady darkness that yielded unwillingly to my candle. The gleam cast rich shadows from the two rows of wine casks trestled along walls that were ornamented with grotesque, varicolored growths. I went at once to the hugest of the casks. Lowering the candle to the antique bench, I held a pewter tankard under the spigot. The turn of the tap in my eager fingers released a smooth stream that shone blood-red. I lifted the brimming tankard to my yearning lips and sent the wine sluicing down my aching throat.

TO the other wines in the other casks I gave not a single thought. They were excellent, full-bodied and delicate of bouquet, but they could not compare with the scarlet nectar that I had drawn. It was for this crimson juice of the vine that I had stolen into the hoary cellar. I emptied the tankard, refilled it, drained it again. Its glow suffused my whole being, easing the torture of my yearning—a yearning that nothing else in existence could satisfy. Gratification, intense and ecstatic, laved my soul.

The voices had returned. Motionless, my tongue trembling with the joy of the wine, I tried to distinguish words that somehow seemed to threaten me. A jungle beast lifts its head to catch a sound of alarm while its talons fasten deeper into its prey lest it be robbed of its food—so I stood, head lifted, the pewter vessel in my clenched hand, striving to read meaning into the subdued tones I heard. They were planning—my wife and my friend—planning, I knew, to deprive me of the wine.

The thought terrified me. To lose this blissful juice, never again to taste its ineffable flavor—I knew it would mean insufferable agony. The longing that always filled me, springing into my vitals the moment I left the great cask, growing stronger and stronger until I returned to slake it at this spigot, was more than mere thirst. It was profounder, more deeply elemental than any thirst a desert traveler could have suffered. It was a need crying up from the primitive well-springs of my being, a longing of my soul and my organs upon which life itself seemed to depend. In all the world nothing could relieve it but the scarlet mercy of this venerable wine. And now they were scheming to rob me of it, to cheat me of the sheerest, most sublime rapture I had ever known!

A cold fury of defiance seized me. I crept back to the door. Carrying the candle, I mounted the worn stone flight that angled up from the darkness of the deep cellar to a rear hallway. Wary and fearful, I drifted to the curtained arch of the library, led by the voices. Clare and Gerry did not know I was close. Concealing myself behind the portieres, my lips still dewed with the wondrous deliciousness of the wine, I listened to them plan.

"You and I," my wife was saying shakenly, "must help him—there's no one else. We must try to understand the ghastly change that's come over Bart. It's the wine that's made him like this. For his own sake, we've got to save him from it, Gerry. I can't help feeling that it goes much deeper, somehow, than merely a craving for drink. But whatever it is we must keep him away from the wine."

"He *has* changed," Gerald Ingram answered. "He's no longer the man you married, Clare, nor my old friend."

I forced back a derisive laugh. They were speaking so soberly, so regretfully, not knowing that I had found in the wine a happiness greater than they had ever dreamed. They were worrying about me while I was experiencing a heavenly joy beyond their conception. What if I had changed? What if I had abandoned my work, what if I no longer joined them in the trivialities that gave them pleasure? Let them say what they liked, I was glad for everything they deplored about me. I lived in a world of beatitude apart from them—I lived for the wine.

Clare was saying softly: "It has poisoned him in so many ways, Gerry. It's made him dissatisfied with everything that used to make us so happy together." Her voice lowered vibrantly. "Bart no longer finds satisfaction in me. He would rather have a goblet of the wine—than me. He

finds something in it that's—that's made him stop loving me."

"Clare!" Gerald Ingram was shocked.

"It's settled, then. There may be hell to pay afterward, but Bart will have no more of that damned wine!"

FILLED with cold fury and colder dread, I crept away. The words I had heard rang in my ears like a sentence of doom—like a decree damning me to a living death, for I knew the torture of my desire, if the wine were gone, would be insufferable, worse by far than the loss of my life. My wife and my best friend —they were not giving me understanding and sympathy, but threatening me with inhuman agony. Desperate to escape it, I hurried to the cellar entrance, ran down the stone stairs into the candle-lighted darkness.

Carrying the taper, I rapidly searched. In the mildewed corners and in ancient racks I found several old jugs. Many parts of the house were still strange to me, for Clare and I had not lived here long, but in my swift hunt I probed into every cranny. I carried the jugs to the huge cask in the underground room— every one I could find. All the while I listened, fevered with the hope that I could finish my task before they came down. When, at last, I was satisfied that there were no more jugs, I shut myself inside the wine cellar, intent on saving every precious drop of the nectar.

I opened the spigot, sent the crimson stream gushing full force into a funnel thrust into the neck of the demijohn. As it filled, frothing with scarlet bubbles, I heeded every slight threat of sound. The moment it was full I turned the red cascade into another vessel and swung the first into a space behind the opposite row of barrels where it could not be seen. Treasuring every blood-colored drop, I worked breathlessly, as fast as the flow allowed, concealing each jug as rapidly as it brimmed.

How narrowly I had missed knowing the ecstacy of this wine! Actually I had allowed a glass of it to go scarcely tasted the first time Clare had poured it for dinner. I had inherited the pre-revolutionary house from my uncle Sebastian Forsythe. My forebears, a strange lot of recluses I had been told, had yearly made wine from the grapes growing lushly over vast tracts at the rear of the estate. The fermented juices of the vines had richened for many years in the ancient tuns in this cellar. To me they had seemed an unimportant acquisition—until that first haunting taste.

The bouquet of the red wine had permeated my mind and all my senses with a growing spell. It possessed a sublime quality alien to all the other vintages. I found myself longing for it with a sharpening thirst that I could not forget. Soon I found myself leaving work to respond to the lure of this blissful draught. At nights I abandoned my bed, yielding to my desire for it. I dreaded the coming of the moment when the great cask would no longer flow. Now, as I crouched beside the streaming tap, sounds in the rooms above menaced me with the loss of my priceless wine.

They were coming down! Nerves burning, I waited while the jug filled. Now a group of them were hidden behind the other barrels. I had saved much of the wine, but some was left in the cask. It was flowing more slowly when footfalls overhead came along the hallway to the cellar entrance. Hearing Clare and Gerry descending the stone flight, I waited until the last second before I turned the handle. Then, dropping the half-filled jug beside the others, I puffed out my candle and climbed into the black space behind the opposite row of barrels.

The swinging door brought the shine of naked flames into the fragrant cavern.

Huddling against the wall that was alive with fungi, I watched my wife and my friend enter.

Suddenly I hated this sweet-faced, russet-haired girl whom I had married—hated her for her purpose. My eyes narrowed at sight of the strong-shouldered, firm-chinned young man at her side. Gerald Ingram was carrying a sledge hammer. He lowered his candle to the bench, gazing grimly at Clare.

She pointed to the cask of the red wine like an executioner indicating a doomed being. Ingram straddled, fastening his hands on the shaft of the implement. Suddenly he drove a powerful blow that splintered the head of the cask. As the thunderous reverberation echoed through the cellar I stifled a mocking laugh. They did not know I had drained most of the wine away! Cradled in its jugs, it lay beside me in the deep shadow, more precious than liquid gold, saved from their heartless destruction.

The heavy sledge slammed into the cask again and again. In torment I heard the splash and drip of some of the wine spilling through the broken wood. I could see Ingram beating the hammer upon the head of the staves, destroying it while scarlet puddles formed on the floor. He drew back, tossing the sledge away, his eyes lighted with triumph.

The fool! He didn't know! And Clare was smiling, tears in her eyes, as though she, too, thought she had won over her rival, the wine. She hurried from the cellar, Ingram after her, and the heavy oaken door thudded shut.

AS I rose from my hiding place, chuckling derisively, I was startled to see the great cask wavering on its trestle. Suddenly it rolled ponderously from its supports, toppling to the floor. The impact caused it to disintegrate. I heard its staves splitting apart, its great hoops clattering down, as I worked my way out of the dark lane. Hurriedly I opened the door to make sure Clare and Gerry had gone. Then, my heart pounding with the assurance that I could save the wine I had jugged, I turned back thirstily to the puddles on the floor. I flung myself flat, tongue avid for the scarlet pools—but on the instant I became motionless, staring in transfixed wonderment.

I was not alone. The fragments of the great cask lay wet in the spilled wine, but it was not at those seasoned pieces of wood that I stared. My eyes clung to a soft, white form dewed with drops of red. She lay as if asleep on a bed of scarlet, her body in gentlest repose. For a moment I was too bewildered, too enchanted to realize where she had come from, but suddenly I knew that the breaking of the cask had revealed her. The staves of her prison, opening under the blows of the sledge, had released her—this woman of the wine!

No breath lifted the young firmness of her breasts. Her lips, redder even than that pool in which she lay, were soundless. Her eyes were closed, the long black lashes shadowing her cheeks. Her dark hair, wet with the wine, clung to her flawless skin. Drops of scarlet clung to her slender flanks. In naked beauty she lay still while, as if in a dream, I brought myself to my feet.

This—this, I told myself, is why I love the wine! This Aphrodite of the vines whose flesh gave savor to the liquid in which she had lain! At that moment I did not wonder what mysterious machinations had placed her inside the cask, or how long the scarlet fluid had washed her perfect body. I knew only that she was young with an eternal youthfulness, beautiful in her nudeness beyond the powers of poets to delineate. And I knew, suddenly and completely, that all the while it was this woman of the wine whom I had de-

sired, whose allure flamed in my blood.

Dead, I moaned. Dead, of course. Perhaps decades ago her body had been concealed in the cask. She was an exquisite being of another age whom the wine had preserved, at last to lay her at my feet.

But—suddenly she was standing before me! I was aware, in a dreamy flash, that she was looking at me, smiling at me. Little rivulets of red caressed her body, trickling down into the pool in which she stood. Hers were dark eyes filled with a haunting luminescence. Her smile was a calm, scarlet beckoning. She was reaching her hand toward me—a hand dainty and slender, wet with the wine, inviting me to an unearthly blissfulness. The girl of the vine was speaking of love with moist, silent lips.

Slowly, transfixed with rapture, I raised my hand toward hers. My fingers poised with the dread that I would feel only empty air; but, gently, I brought them trembling to her. I felt the winey clasp of her hand! Then, swiftly, fleet as the nymph she was, she sprang away. The candlelight glistened over her luscious body as she fled into the dark shadows in the corner.

A hoarse protest broke from my thirsty lips and I bounded after her. I closed my arms around—not around the firm suppleness of her, not around her lithesome, fragrant flesh—but around nothingness, emptiness!

She was gone! I stood a moment, staring at the blank stone wall I faced. The ancient rocks that composed it were covered with their crust of growths, unbroken. The old mortar mocked me with its solidity. Abruptly, thinking that the girl had hidden exactly as I had concealed myself, I looked behind the casks. None of the shadows sheltered her. Though I sought her in every possible place, I did not find her. She seemed to have eluded me by passing through the wall of stone. I told myself, then, that my eyes had tricked me, that I had imagined her.

But, looking at the earthen floor, at the edge of the pool where the wine had softened the black dirt, I found a print of her naked foot.

CHAPTER TWO

Vina

VOICES upstairs startled me. In my sudden apprehension to save the wine I had jugged, I turned away. Hurrying from the wine-cellar, I groped to the rear of the basement and there quietly opened the bulkhead. Returning I hooked two of the heavy jugs in each hand, then climbed out into the night. I wanted to find some place to hide the priceless treasure.

Then a call shocked a chill of alarm through me. It came across the grounds, floating through the moonlight from the adjacent estate. It was a man's voice, quavering with age, strained with pleading, that stopped me short in the darkness. It called:

"Vina! . . . Vina! . . ."

It was Gillian Albernon. My neighbor was a white-headed man, infirm with age, who lived alone in the moldering house across the wall. Before senescence had claimed him, he had achieved some acclaim as an artist. I had read that at the height of his career his talents had, somehow, failed him, for his later canvases had been scorned. I felt sorry for him because his genius had broken so unaccountably, but tonight, anxious to hide the jugs, I cursed him.

"Vina!" he called plaintively. "Vina!"

I had reason to think the old man was mad. This had happened many times before. On moonlit evenings I had found him wandering through the shadows, crawling over the walls, invading my own property, with the name Vina quavering

from his lips. I had been told that this was the name of a girl he had loved in his youth. Long ago, the story went, she had died, but he could not believe it, and when he was most miserably lonesome in the fullness of the moon he prowled the hills, searching for her. I had learned to humor him by ignoring him but tonight, anxious to avoid discovery, I burned with impatience.

"Vina!" he called.

He was drifting through my garden. I could see his white head, his piteous eyes seeking his beloved in the darkness. As he groped on, I hurried from the bulkhead, along a path that led into the vineyards. At one point near the wall rocks were tumbled into a high mound. I found a hollow behind them which could serve as a perfect storage place for the wine. I slid the jugs into it, then hurried back for the others.

"Vina!" Gillian Albernon's voice whimpered on the wind as he continued his wretched search. "Vina! . . ."

Alert against observation, I hastened back and forth between the wine-cellar and the heap of rocks, transferring my scarlet hoard. At last my task was completed. With a stone I closed the hollow that contained riches greater than any pirate loot. Dizzied with relief, I drifted back to the house, tantalized by a memory of the exquisite being I had seen among the casks—the nymph of the vine. I returned to the wine-cellar, bringing my candle close to the rim of the pool in the cellar.

The light still revealed the clear-cut print of a girl's bare foot.

Troubled, mystified, my eyes aching to see this lovely creature again, my hand eager to return to hers, I puffed out the flame and left the basement by way of the bulkhead. Wishing Clare and Gerry to believe I was unaware of what they had done, lest they uncover my cache and destroy my wine, I went back into the house by the side door. I found them in the library. They ceased talking when I entered. Fearing my enmity might blaze out of my eyes, I looked away from them to study the oil portrait hanging above the fireplace.

It seemed to be a painting of myself. Its every feature, its every shade of coloring were mine. Each time I looked at the picture I marveled, for the likeness to me was so remarkably close I might have been gazing into a mirror. Actually it depicted my grandfather, whose name I bear. Gillian Albernon had executed the portrait at the height of his career. The Hobart Forsythe in the frame had lain buried these many years in the little private cemetery at the rear of the estate which is bordered by the abundant foliage of the vineyard.

My namesake, I recalled, had brought disgrace to a proud family. As a child I had overheard a few of the scandalous details without understanding them. Since inheriting the old house and coming here to complete my book, I had learned a little more from a number of old letters I had found in the attic.

My grandfather, after marrying, and while my uncle and my father were still boys, had fallen in love with a girl who had come from I know not where. I had heard her described as ravishingly beautiful even by those who hated her. The culmination of the affair was that my grandmother, with her two sons, had been forced to abandon her home. The first Hobart Forsythe had then brought his mistress to this house. Under the moral code of the day they were righteously shunned by all the churchly who had been grandfather's friends. They had become joyous pariahs together, content to live apart from the rest of the world in an Eden of their own.

I did not know what had become of the first Hobart Forsythe's beautiful mistress. There is no record of her death. No headstone in the cemetery bore a name that could be hers. The physician who had come to minister to my grandfather when he was dying had found him wretchedly alone, with no hint of a woman's presence in the house. Until tonight I had never been able to find a hint to the mystery of that lovely woman's fate, but as I gazed at the old oil portrait my blood tingled with a weird chill.

The girl of the wine!

CLARE broke the uncanny spell of my fascination by speaking at that moment. She came quickly to my side, taking my arm. "Bart, darling," she said quietly. "I've an idea. It's a long time since we've been away. Let's get in the car and go somewhere—anywhere. Let's just drive and have a grand time going places, as we used to do. We can be packed and ready inside an hour."

I looked at her intently. I was still in love with her, in a way, yet it was not the same as before. Something remained because I had known Clare longer than I can remember. Though something powerful had come between us, she was fighting to break down the barrier because, I knew, she still loved me as much as she always had. Her suggestion was an attempt to reclaim me. Her eyes pleaded as she spoke.

"Splendid idea, Bart!" Gerry Ingram said with excessive enthusiasm. "Hop off with Clare for a while, and when you come back you'll feel your old self. I'll help you get your things together, old timer."

Gerald Ingram had been my roommate at Dartmouth. We had grown closer than blood brothers, even after my writing and Gerry's studies in psychiatry had taken us along divergent paths. I had always looked forward to his occasional visits, but this time he seemed to be part of a world I had renounced. Clare and Gerry were no longer inhabitants of my sphere. I didn't belong with them any more, because I belonged with—with the wine.

"No," I answered flatly. I knew clearly enough what it would mean. It would separate me from my jugs of scarlet ambrosia and bring me unsufferable torment. Every mile and every minute would pile up into torture greater than I could endure. Both fear of that agony, and thirst for the bliss of the wine, prompted my point-blank refusal. Even now the yearning was growing within me—the longing was sharpening so that soon I must yield to the lure of the cool liquid sweetness. I said with finality: "I won't even consider going away."

"Bart, darling." Clare beseechingly took my arms. "What is it? Is it that you don't love me at all any more? Is there something that means more to you now—than I? Tell me—open up your heart to me. I want to help you. You must know I'll do anything for you, darling—anything."

Even as she spoke I was thinking of the girl of the wine—of the white, naked, wine-wet body which had risen from its pool of red to beckon me to ineffable joy. I could not tell Clare that. It was hopeless to try to make her understand. Clare could know nothing of the desire pulsing in my blood. The mere thought of the inexpressibly beautiful woman of the cask set a flame inside me.

Where was she? Where had she gone? Would she come back, or had I lost her forever?

I turned from Clare wordlessly, left Gerry staring. I hurried from the house, ran into the darkness. In the moonlight I sought the alluring, nameless being. I hunted through the shadows, my eyes and my arms and my whole organism hungry for her. I forgot the whole world in my eagerness to find her. I told myself she must be near, waiting for me. . . .

A call brought me to a pause. "Vina! . . . Vina! . . ." It was the lonesome, quavering cry of the hoary-headed Gillian Albernon. I saw the old man, a dark figure in the garden. He was following the path, the moon glinted in his piteous eyes which could not see that the past years were no more, that the love he had found in them had withered forever and was gone. I stood still while his infirm legs took him along the path, until he disappeared in the gloom.

Then a gentle, soft rustle of leaves quickened my heart. It was not the sound of the wind in the foliage that shivered along my nerves. It was the noise of a presence among the vines that twined over the silvered hillside. I looked with hopeful fascination at a ripe cluster of grapes swinging slowly. Fingers stole around them—white, slender fingers—tightening. I saw the crushed grapes yield juice that bathed the closing hand. Then the stem snapped, and a dark opening appeared, framing a face. . . .

Her face was shining with ruby droplets, as though she had been drenched in a rain of wine. Her fulgent eyes were upon me, drawing me closer. Dimly outlined behind the leaves, her firm, ripe body was shadowed. Her red, wet mouth was lifted through the opening in the vine—lifting for mine.

Because I feared she was a vision that might vanish I dared not touch her, but I brought my yearning mouth closer to her lips . . . gently closer. One instant I felt their touch—one instant I caught their heady bouquet—then, swiftly, she was gone, with the sweetness of the wine left upon my lips.

Gone—but there was a fleet movement in the vineyard, a lithe white form flashing through the gloom with the nimbleness of a doe. The glistening nakedness of the girl of the wine lured me after her. I could see her, a misty dream creature, silently running. But abruptly, she halted. She poised, outlined in the moonlight, as a voice cried out of the night:

"Vina! Vina!"

Gillian Albernon was stumbling toward her. His white hair tore in the wind, his old eyes shone wildly as his gnarled arms groped for her. Plaintive sobs broke from his cracked throat as he tottered to a stop, reaching to enclose her in a longing embrace. "Vina!" he choked out with delirious jubilation. "Vina, my beloved!" Then, at the instant when his arms almost caught her, she whisked away.

She bounded, her long wine-splashed legs flashing. She fled into the obscurity of a shadow while the feeble old man tottered after her. He beat the leaves in search for her, calling her name miserably again and again. I could hear him sobbing with despair until, suddenly, he stumbled away. He broke into a limping run across the garden, driven by a sudden despondency that wrung hideous moans from him. Wavering in the direction of his home, he disappeared.

I LET him go. I went on quietly, searching for the woman of the wine. I knew she would come again, knew there was an affinity that bound me to her, but I wished not to frighten her with haste. The lingering taste of her delectable lips on mine led me along the stone wall, my eyes starving for the glimpse I knew must come. But abruptly, again, I paused. I stared at a looming black shadow on the high, broad window of Gillian Albernon's studio.

He was standing near the blinded panes, one arm lifted—pressing the muzzle of a gun to his temple!

An exclamation of horror broke from my throat. I vaulted the wall, flung myself into a run that took me to Albernon's door. Heaving in, I saw him still standing rigid beside an easel, light streaming upon

him, his blue-lidded eyes closed, tightening himself to pull the trigger.

"Drop that!"

At my ringing command he spun about. I snatched at the revolver, but he was quick enough in his desperation to evade me. He stumbled against the wall, turning the weapon upon me so fiercely that I jerked myself to a stop. One twitch of his palsied finger, I knew, might drop me dead on the spot. I drew back, but the weapon remained pointing waveringly at my heart. His drawn lips worked out breathless words:

"Once we were the same age, you and I—but you are still young, Hobart Forsythe, and I am old now—old. . . ."

This poor old man's rheumy eyes, I told myself, were deceiving him. He believed me to be the Hobart Forsythe who was dead, had spoken to me as though to my grandfather. I realized that in the distress of his madness Gillian Albernon must be thinking that all the world had remained as it had been two generations ago while he alone had aged. He stared at me wretchedly, still pointing the gun at my heart, while his sagging face writhed in torture.

"She, too, is young—young as when I last saw her. God! it seems centuries since that night when she left me. But she has not changed. She is still a beautiful girl, but I—I am a doddering, toothless scarecrow now. That is why she fled from me —why she will always be revolted by the sight of me. All these years I have waited for her, and called to her to come back, but I know it is hopeless—hopeless—"

I said quietly: "Put down that gun."

He did not hear. "I knew she didn't really love me, Hobart Forsythe, even when she gave herself to me that night. I think it was pity that made her do it, because she knew I loved her so desperately. But all the while her heart was yours. You are the man she loved then, the man she still loves. God! to have lived all these lonely years since I saw her last —to learn this!"

I could not speak.

"I thought—I thought—" the old artist's frayed voice quavered on—"you had killed her. I thought you had taken her life because you suspected she had been unfaithful with me, but now I know you forgave her. You have kept her hidden and to yourself this long while. Your love has made you youths together while I have shriveled and weakened. My love for Vina has not withered, but it is over now—over!"

So swiftly that I could not stop him, he swung the gun back to his temple. Though I sprang toward him, desperate to snatch the revolver away, he pressed the muzzle to his head before I could touch it. Fierce fire gushed from the barrel to singe his hair as a deafening report shocked through the studio. Gillian Albernon moaned as he dropped into my arms. Scarcely a drop of blood flowed from the round, burned hole, because instantly he was dead.

Stunned, my heart pounding, I lowered him to the couch. I tore a tapestry from the wall to cover him. Turning away, troubled bewilderment storming inside me, I caught sight of the canvas on the easel. I had noticed, when visiting this studio during the past months, that always the easel was draped as though to cover the work in progress, though Albernon had not touched a brush in years. Now the canvas was bared. I gazed transfixed at the painting—at the lifelike, full length figure of a nude girl of exquisite beauty.

The girl of the wine! It was her softly modelled face, her smouldering eyes, her ripe mouth! The firm curves of the unclad body were hers. Hers were the breasts I had seen dewed with scarlet wine in the pool of the broken cask. The flesh-tones of the oils glowed with radiant life against an incompleted background. This was the painting that had marked the end of a great artist's career. This was the woman of the vine—*Vina!*

CHAPTER THREE

Vineyard Paradise

I GAZED wordless at the incredibly lovely creature depicted on the canvas. The sight brought an intense burning to my throat, aroused a desire that flamed through my blood. The scarlet temptation thirsted within me, mounting to an unbearable pitch, as I tore myself away. I hurried out the door, forgetting everything else in my intense craving for the wine. I sprang over the, wall, raced across the garden. Dropping to a crouch beside the mound of rock where I had hidden the jugs, I reached in avidly—reached into emptiness!

The jugs were gone!

Dim in the moonlight, a supple, silvered figure—she was drifting toward me. Her eyes were shining with gladness, her body swaying with easy grace at each step. Her red mouth shone moistly in the glow —gleamed with the fragrant wetness of the wine she had drunk. She was holding one of the jugs in her hands, extending it to bestow its appeasement upon me. She stood silent, still smiling, as I grasped it and poured the scarlet deliciousness down my parched throat.

I looked upon her, seeing that her softly patrician features were those that the brush of Gillian Albernon had depicted two generations ago, and I understood. I knew that the first Hobart Forsythe had discovered the unfaithfulness of Vina with the artist, had imprisoned her in the wine in the cask. The staves had held her captive these seven decades while she fed upon the wine and the wine preserved her in all her ripe youthfulness. For her there was no time and now, for me, too, there was only timelessness—for I was the living embodiment of the love she had borne my grandfather. Hobart Forsythe was dead and moldering in his grave, yet Hobart Forsythe was alive and young and hungering. . . .

My fingertips drew lightly over her wine-wet skin. I turned from the jug to the creature who had imparted her allure to it. She drew back gently as my hands closed upon her shoulders. My palms pressed downward, softly, gently, to enclose her in a devouring embrace. She yielded, yet resisted, as my arms twined about her, as the bouquet of her being flooded into my lungs and dizzied my mind. She was coming to me . . . coming. . . .

Until a voice called sharply from the house: "Bart! Where are you, Bart?"

Instantly Vina flashed from my arms. She bounded into the shadow of a lilac bush with graceful agility, and there she stood trembling with fright, the droplets on her body twinkling like jewels in the moonlight. I inwardly raged at the interruption that had robbed me of her. Footfalls were following the path. I neither moved toward him nor retreated as Gerry Ingram neared. He paused, smiling ingratiatingly, to say quietly:

"We were wondering what happened to you, Bart. Clare is worried, you know. How about joining us inside?"

The name of my wife was a foreign sound, like the name of a stranger. It was meaningless in the turmoil of longing that filled me. I did not even glance at Ingram because I could not take my gaze from the statuesque figure obscured in the gloom. I sensed that he was peering in the same direction. A proud exaltation filled me, a determination to break all other ties so that nothing could stand between Vina and me. I said in a whisper:

"Do you see her—standing there in the dark?"

He answered after a moment: "Yes."

"Her name is Vina," I told him. "You have never seen any other woman so beautiful. Never in all the world, since the beginning of time, has there been another woman to compare with her. I love her—love her as she loves me. There is nothing else in all the universe but our love for each other. She will come to me soon—come to remain in my arms for ever."

Ingram asked in a low tone: "Is it love for you she feels, or love of love itself?"

I smiled at the absurdity of his question. The bond uniting Vina and me had been forged by the decades. Our adoration had sprung into being long before I was born. My worship of her was a heritage bred into my blood. Three score and ten years it had endured. The same timeless flame burned in both Vina and me— a hot flame that could never die. I answered Ingram confidently:

"It could not possibly be the same for her with any other man—not possibly."

THEN I sensed him moving. Startled, I saw him drifting toward the shadow that clothed Vina. She stood poised to bound away, but his steps were so slow, so quiet, they did not frighten her. He extended his hand toward her. I heard him whisper, "Vina— come to me, Vina." He was an advancing shadow from which she did not flee. I saw a a bright, exultant light spring into her eyes as he paused before her.

I realized in grieved dismay that he was taking her into his arms. He was drawing her glistening body, as I yearned to do, close to him. I saw her resisting a little, yet she was yielding. His embrace was enclosing her. Suddenly I was thinking that he was taking her away from me. Rage burst into my heart with violent heat. I sprang forward with fists clenched, filled with an ungovernable savage fury. "Get away from her!"

I gripped Ingram's shoulder, tore him back, Vina sprang out of his arms, retreating against the leaves. She stood silent, with eyes glowing, as I spun Ingram to face me. Insane jealousy of him aroused a tempest within me. I thrust him away, every muscle tight with wrath. He checked himself, straddling, his eyes glinting narrowed into mine.

"Don't ever touch her again!" I warned him. "She belongs to me—to me, do you hear?"

He uttered a short, sardonic laugh. "I mean to take her away from you, Bart," he answered. "I mean to make her my own."

"By God—!"

I struck him with all my strength. I drove my clenched fist full into his face. The blow staggered him, but he steadied himself, peering at me banefully. He flung himself at me. His fists smashed at my eyes. I was aware, as we struggled, that Vina was still huddling under the leaves, watching us. Filled with the mad purpose of proving to her that no man could take her from me, I lashed at Gerald Ingram with crushing fury.

He dropped into the grass, but instant-he drew up, throwing himself into a fiercer attack. I met it squarely, jarring him back on his heels. I knew nothing but that I must beat him down, drive him away—this man who had once been my closest friend. The savagery of my blows compelled him to retreat. I shocked him back, step by step, pounding my knuckles into his face. Suddenly he sprawled backward. Suddenly, with a loud splintering sound, he disappeared into the darkness.

For a moment I stood hunched, fists still ready, without realizing what had happened. Then I heard a far-away rippling of water, and felt dank air gusting upon me, and I knew. Ingram had fallen across the head of the cistern. The

old boards of the housing had broken under him. He had plunged into the depths of the cavity.

Then a splashing sound reached my ears. A muffled, reverberating voice called up: "Bart! Bart!" I did not answer. The water in the cistern, I knew, was at low level, perhaps not deeper than Ingram's waist. He had pulled himself up from the bottom, was groping around the cylindrical walls which offered him no means of lifting himself. Listening to the sounds of his movements, I reflected that the cistern was never used, that it was not near the house. When he called again— "Bart! Can you hear me, Bart?"—I snarled down at him:

"You'll never steal her away from me now—never!"

Straightening, I looked into the shadow. She was still there, watching me with her lustrous eyes. Vina was smiling at me. I yearned to go to her, to enwrap her wine-sparkled body in my arms, but I was still envenomed with mad jealousy. Upon sudden thought, I loped away from the broken housing toward a little shack sitting at the entrance of the vineyard.

"Bart!" Ingram's hollow voice called faintly again. "Throw me a rope, Bart!"

Grimly I fastened my hands upon the ears of two fat bags of soil dressing that were stored in the shack. I dragged them back, plumped them down at the edge of the broken boards. Ignoring Ingram's pleading shouts, I retraced my steps, returning with two more bags. I piled them on top of the others, and continued until the shattered cistern-head was completely covered. When I paused, at last, simmering with sweat, the hollow was sealed—Ingram's voice was blotted away save for the faintest echo.

"You'll never take her from me!"

ALL the while Vina had watched. I went toward her gently, thirstily. My exertion had sharpened my craving for the dulcet wine, yet Vina's nearness meant profounder gratification. My arms reached for her as I glided into the shadow. Though her silent, red lips invited me, she drew back with her wine-wet skin passing glistening under my fingers. I saw her pointing—pointing wordlessly toward the house. I did not understand the message in her glimmering eyes, but I looked in the direction she indicated.

A silhouetted figure had appeared in the French windows. Clare was coming out. She came along the path, looking about. "Bart!" she called. "Gerry! Where are you?" As she came closer, Vina's arm slipped through my moist hand. The girl of the wine drew deeper into the darkness, still pointing toward Clare. Now in Vina's eyes there gleamed a command. I could not read its meaning then, but I knew it was inexorable, somehow imposing upon me a requirement I must meet.

Suddenly she was gone. Suddenly there was only the wine wetness on my hand. I turned away as Clare approached along the path. Clare was still calling, "Gerry! Bart! Are you all right?" She could not hear the faint ringing of Ingram's voice in the sealed cistern but, fearing that her ears might catch it, I hurried out of the shadow to meet her and draw her away. She stopped short when I appeared, and responded at once to my grip upon her arms as I started toward the house with her.

She said: "Something's happened! Where is Gerry? What is it, Bart?"

I did not answer. I led her into the library. Blinking in the light, I faced her.

"Bart," she said quietly. "There's nothing that can ever really separate us. No matter what happens to you, no matter where you go, I want to be at your side, always. If this—if this is something I can share, please let me share it with you. I don't care what becomes of me

as long as we're together, completely, in everything."

Suddenly I felt sorry for Clare. She was fighting to keep everything she held dearest in the world—fighting her utmost, fearlessly, against a force she knew was overwhelming. Her unflinching resolution, her unselfishness, touched me deeply. I drew her gently close to me and put my arms around her. She held me tight, her head lowered to my shoulder. I could feel her sobbing inwardly. She whispered:

"You're my life, Bart, my whole life."

A flicker of motion raised my eyes. My gaze turned to the window. Outside the panes I saw a white, red-touched face gazing in. It was Vina. The eyes of the girl of the wine were fixed upon me. The softness in them was gone—instead of the unearthly luminosity there was a fierce, angry blaze. Her inviting mouth had become forbidding. I knew instantly it was because I had, for the moment, gone back to Clare.

Swiftly I tore my arms away from Clare, stepping from her. Startled, she searched my face, then looked toward window. The dark-framed features of Vina were still visible behind the glass. My withdrawal from Clare had lighted triumph in the wine-woman's eyes. She faded back into the darkness. The sounds of running feet rustled out of the night. With a soft moan of yearning breaking from my throat, I started after her.

"Bart!" Clare's hand was on my arm. "Don't go, Bart!"

I wrenched free of Clare's fingers. I sprang out into the gloom. Vina was lost in it now, but I could hear a faint fluttering of leaves that told me she was waiting for me somewhere in the vineyard. Hurrying along the path, I sought her.

She was standing, a silver-white figure flecked with scarlet, among the green leaves. I went toward her gently. She did not move as I drifted toward her. Her motionlessness as I raised my arms was surrender. My mind reeled with the ecstasy of a dream come true as I felt her cool, naked softness within my embrace. I took the nectar of her wine-red lips for a long moment of transported bliss. Then, suddenly, she slipped away.

The fierceness was again in her eyes as she pointed toward the house. Her extended arm expressed the same inexorable command. This time I understood her wordlessness. I realized that Vina would never give herself to me as long as any barrier stood between us. I knew that Vina and I were separated by Clare's existence. The living woman was intolerable to the girl of the vine. Vina's extended finger was commanding me—to kill.

CHAPTER FOUR

Cup of Death

I TURNED from Vina because I knew, with the finality of doom, that my arms could never hold her until I had met her merciless requirement. Flaming exaltation, blood red, filled Vina's eyes as I strode to the path. I felt her following me as I went back to the house. Her bare wet feet were soundless in the grass, but I knew she meant to watch until I had fulfilled her demand. Then. . . . God! The thought of the fruition to follow set my heart heaving hotly. The promised rapture fired me with unreasoning obsession. I flung myself to the entrance of the library, an inferno of savage purpose, fuming within me.

On the sill I stopped short. Clare was standing in the far corner of the room, her back turned. She was speaking over the telephone. She was saying:

"I've hoped so desperately that it wouldn't be necessary, Dr. Blanchard, but now I know there is no alternative. I'm afraid—terribly afraid. Will you come—come immediately?"

Those few words whipped me into a fiercer rage. I knew Dr. Blanchard. He was the director of the sanitarium which sat a mile farther down the road. It was an institution for the mentally deranged, high-fenced, guarded, a regimented prison for the mad. Clare had summoned Dr. Blanchard to seize me. She was going to throw me into that howling bedlam of the demented. In this way she meant to wall me away from Vina!

The breaking of a snarl from my lips startled Clare so that she dropped the telephone and recoiled against the wall. She stood rigid, her trembling hand lifted to her parted lips. I knew she was reading my purpose in my blazing eyes. The mute terror that gripped her told me she knew —knew I was going to kill her.

I went toward her, slow step after slow step, my clawed hands lifting. Transfixed, she watched me. In abysmal fright she shrank against the wall. I paused directly in front of her, my fingers hooking to take her throat. Then a scream broke from her lips. She flung herself hysterically upon me. The force of her fear struck me back. I stumbled, tottered against a chair, sprawled to the floor. As I scrambled crazily to get up I heard her running. When I regained my feet she was gone, but my purpose remained—my determination to murder her.

"Clare!"

My torn voice echoed from the long hall. No sound signaled me Claire's hiding-place. Looking out the French windows, I knew instantly she had not fled that way, because I saw a face dim in the gloom. Vina's—she was out there in the darkness, watching. The faint whiteness of Vina's nude body blended away in the night as my eyes hungered for it. I tore away, striding along the hall to the rear of the house.

Stepping into the darkness, I paused on the porch, grimly searching. Almost unconsciously my fingers strayed to the handle of a sickle hanging in its place among a few garden tools. I clenched the curved blade, starting out. Abruptly a cry chilled me. It was Clare's voice. Swift, running footfalls mingled with the echoes —light sounds rustling the grass, made by Vina's bare feet. I sprang away, hurrying along the wall until I paused with my infuriate eyes upon Clare.

She was standing at a spot where the vines grew thickly over the stones. In one of her hands she was holding a jug. She had heard my approach—she was gazing at me wildly. As she stood motionless, I looked past her to another figure, dim as a dream in the darkness. Farther back, Vina was huddled. With a cold start I realized what had happened. Escaping the house, Clare had glimpsed Vina. She had followed Vina. She had found the wine.

Clare lifted the jug to her lips. A sob broke from them as they parted for the wine. She poured a scarlet stream into her throat. It trickled from her mouth, streaked down her neck. She was madly devouring precious stuff that belonged only to Vina and to me! I lurched at her, snarling at her to stop. I snatched the jug out of her hands, quaking with fury. She turned upon me, her lips red.

"Please!" she said. "I want it to do to me what it's done to you, Bart—so that it will bring us closer together instead of separate us. Let me drink the wine!"

My lips curled scornfully. "This is not for you! This is my love for Vina, and Vina's for me. You can't trespass—can't rob us of the wine. You can't—come between us."

AT my slow step she glimpsed the sickle clenched in my fist. The ominous gleam of its blade shot new terror through her. She recoiled, her one hand closing hard upon her bodice. Suddenly, possessed

with her heedless determination she ripped at her dress. She tore it off her, slipped out of her silk. In a moment she was standing naked before me. She reached down into the shadows of the vines and caught up another of the jugs.

"I will!" she whispered huskily. "The wine will make you want me as you want her. Look at me—watch me drink it!"

"Stop!" I shouted at her. "Don't take another drop! It's not for you, I tell you! You can never take Vina's place—never!"

She choked out: "Then—"

She hurled the jug away. It struck the stone wall and burst. Its fragments fell clattering while foaming crimson cascaded over the rocks. Seeing the precious nectar streaming, I stood in a paralysis of wrath.

Shattering concussions froze me. Then I saw Clare seizing one after another of the priceless jugs. She was smashing them rapidly against the wall! Out of the darkness Vina had sprung. The girl of the vine was frenziedly pulling at Clare's arms, straining to prevent the wanton spilling of the ambrosia. Vina's delicate body was not strong enough to restrain Clare. The jugs were cracking, the wine spattering down. As I lurched toward the two naked bodies I saw that Clare was desperately heaving the last of the vessels.

It smashed with a dull, doomful impact. I realized that there was one other —the jug I had taken from Clare at the beginning and lowered to the ground— but blind rage overpowered me with the thought that Clare had destroyed the wine. I lifted the sickle, straining to strike. She shrank back, falling against the drenched wall, crying wordlessly for mercy. With one fierce explosion of wrath I slashed the blade upon her.

Red streamed over her face—red that was not wine—and she lay huddled, motionless.

Vina sprang away. Whirling, I saw her

catching up the one jug that remained. With a flash of her eyes enticing me, she ran into the vineyard. Starving for her, I raced after her into the deep shadows at the rear of the vine-yard.

Vina paused, turning with the jug in her hand. She was smiling when she swung about but suddenly an expression of un-utterable horror swept over her face. A shattering sound stopped me short. I stared in freezing dismay, realizing that Vina had unwittingly brought the jug into violent contact with the headstone beside which she was poised. It had broken. The wine—the last of the wine—was stream-ing down the time-eaten granite—pouring over the graven name of Hobart Forsythe!

Suddenly, paralyzed as I was at seeing the final drops of the wine falling upon the grave, I was aware that Vina was laugh-ing. No sound came from her lips, but her body was shaking with a proxysm of sardonic raillery. Her eyes blazed with a malevolent light I had never seen before as she silently mocked me. And then— and then the ultimate horror!

Vina's body was changing before my eyes! Its firm, ripe youthfulness was transforming itself into flabbiness that swiftly grew looser, enfolding her in ugly wrinkles. Her face withered and dr ed, her eyes lost lustre as they sank into their sockets. In a moment she was a shriveled, toothless hag—a hideous witch still mock-ing me with silent laughter.

Abruptly this ghastly being dropped to the earth. I stood rooted, seeing it shrink-ing even more. The skin that once had been so lovely with its jewels of wine-drops now was yellowed parchment puck-ered over a scrawny frame. This thing was rotting before my eyes. It became a revolting mass of putrescence. Then, abomination upon abomination, the skele-ton appeared through the crawling putri-faction of the flesh. The body of the girl

of the vine was now a heap of dust eddy-ing away on the night wind.

I choked back a shout of revulsion. Suddenly I found myself running out of the cemetery, through the graveyard. I dropped to my knees beside the still, white body of Clare. I called her name, but my answer was the silence of the night. I took her into my arms, shuddering with grief. Then I realized that the blade of my sickle had merely parted the skin on her forehead. I felt her heart beating.

Crushing her to me, I thanked God with a prayer. I was still holding her, mad with gladness that I had not lost her, when the men from the sanitarium came. . . .

* * *

I brought the car to a stop at the en-trance of the old house. Our trip was over. Clare and Gerry and I had been away a month, touring with happy-go-lucky aim-lessness, and we had completely recap-tured all the joyous comraderie we had ever known. Clare and I had been gay as kids who had just fallen in love, yet at the bottom of my mind, there was a disturbing wonder that distressed me.

I had forgotten my stay in the sani-tarium—forgotten the wet packs and the continuous baths and the confinement. I had been assured by Dr. Blanchard that my condition had been caused by the vicious circle of alcoholic toxicity and nervous exhaustion. I was completely new again. More than Dr. Blanchard's treat-ment, my soul was lightened by the for-giveness of Clare and Gerry.

"My own damned fault, Bart," Gerry had said, "because I did such a bungling job of it. I thought by playing up to your hallucination I could get you out of it. That's why, of course, I pretended to see the girl. She was purely a figment of your imagination that I wanted to win away from you. Served me right, and certainly there are no hard feelings."

He had not, he said, seen Vina. Clare

had not seen her. Was all this, I asked myself, the vision of a drugged mind? Of course it was, they had said. Gerry had shown me, in substantiation, a passage from Noyes' "Modern Clinical Psychiatry" dealing with my ailment:

"Occasionally a mentally overtaxed person may on partaking of even a small amount of alcohol suffer from a striking and severe but transitory mental state known as pathological intoxication. This morbid condition is in effect a dream state suddenly produced by alcohol. The emotional disturbances are profound. The patient is confused, suffers from hallucinations of sight—"

I wondered. Immediately excusing myself from Clare and Gerry, I walked alone into the vineyard. Near the wall I could find no traces of broken jugs—but, I thought, the caretaker might have removed them. I recalled, as I went into the cemetery, that Gillian Abernon had, in fact, committed suicide. Pausing at the grave of the first Hobart Forsythe, I looked at the mound. I saw no bones.

But, I remembered as I turned back, there had been a series of long, heavy rains which might have washed away the remains of Vina's once exquisite body. I could only conjecture, but I was swayed toward concluding that the girl of the vine was a dream creature—until I went into the old wine-cellar.

I paused at the molded oaken door, my one hand on the latch, a candle in the other, hesitating to enter. Its fungus growths glittered as I swung it open ponderously. The gleam of my candle cut through darkness that had not been disturbed since that night of bliss and horror. The fragments of the great, broken cask lay on dark earth from which the pool of wine had long since faded. Heart pounding, I stepped into the corner, stooping to bring the brightest light upon the spot where I had first seen Vina vanish.

The print of her naked foot was there.

THE END

IN OUR NEXT ISSUE!

A tiny strip of paper was glued to the acorn. Upon it
were printed ten words. They were addressed to him -
yet he had entered this room but moments ago! Ten word
which seemed to scream their death message into the
ringing silence:
> STEPHEN BENEDICT, IN ONE MINUTE YOU ARE GOING TO
> DIE.

Scowling, the detective tested the two window locks,
found them both secured and returned to the desk. He
slumped into the chair, drummed his fingers on the
walnut. More seconds ticked by.
Then, impulsively he jerked down the telephone, lifted
the receiver to his ear and thumped the hook up and
down. There was no click, no answering hum! The line
was dead. He replaced the receiver. Revolver in
hand, heart pounding, he waited...
It came like a vision out of hell. Benedict turned
and felt his body suddenly jerk taut. A cold piece
of ice shot up and down his spine.
Framed in the soot-smeared window, leering at him with
huge pupil-less eyes, was the face of a monster! It
was utterly hideous, a semi-human, semi-anthropoid
horror face, bloated five times out of proportion,
covered with black, matted hair. The mouth was a
gaping hole, crowded with yellow fanglike teeth. The
skin gleamed a leprous slate-gray. From the nostrils
protruded a sharpened piece of bone. Draped around
the swollen head was the body of a dead snake.
For a split second the thing remained there, motionless
Then a hairy hand shot upward, struck at the window.
The glass crashed and fell inward ...

A CRUSHED BODY AND A GRINNING DEATH'S-HEAD LED
STEPHEN BENEDICT TO A NIGHT OF HORROR IN A HOUSE OF
HELL - WHERE HANGING CORPSES LOOKED WITH SIGHTLESS
EYES UPON SUCH SCENES AS WOULD HAVE DRIVEN LIVING
MEN INSANE!

A classic novelette of terror by Carl Jacobi, " Satan's
Roadhouse" will be reprinted complete in our 2nd issue
of WEIRD-MENACE CLASSICS. Order now, $5 a copy, from
Robert Weinberg, 10606 S. Central Park, Chicago, Il 60€